WHEN THE SONG VANISHES

WRITTEN BY

KURT JAMES

DEDICATION:
I would like to dedicate this book to my brother
Dane. From the time I was little, he in his way
always protected me from a childhood that had
more unpleasant memories than pleasant ones. He
was and still is my hero.

ACKNOWLEDGMENTS:
I want to thank my lifelong friend and fellow
Sheridan Ram Kurt "Wally" Wollenweber who
without his continuing support I could not fulfill
my dream of being a storyteller.

Disclaimer:
This is a work of fiction. Names, characters,
businesses, places, events and incidents are either
the products of the author's imagination or used in
a fictitious manner. Any resemblance to actual
persons, living or dead, or actual events is purely
coincidental.

KURT JAMES

CHAPTER 1

As I merged onto West Portal road from Highway 34 into the village of Grand Lake, Colorado, the 350 cubic inches of raw power of my Grand County Sheriff K5 1975 Chevy Blazer purred almost silently as Nickey and I drove to Grand Avenue.

Finally pulling up in front of the small one-story barn wood sided bank at 902 Grand Avenue, I turned to look at Nickey - the former Nickey Lynn Chavez - who was now known as Mrs. Nickey Lynn Lee, my wife. She was also a deputy for the Grand County Sheriff's department. As she was filling out a check deposit slip, I asked, "Since Grand Mountain Bank has a branch in Granby, why exactly did we drive fifteen miles to the branch here to deposit your check?"

Nickey, without looking up as she used her math skills to add the numbers in the right-hand column of the deposit slip, said in an almost sneer, "I don't like that female teller at the branch in Granby."

Thinking on that for a second, I spoke. I should have shut up, but I asked, "You mean Kimberly?"

Having completed her deposit slip and after signing the back of her payroll check, Nickey clicked her ballpoint pen loudly as she now looked at me with a half-smile and said, "Yes, the redheaded Kimberly. She has been a snotty bitch to me ever since you and I got married. Did you date 'Kimberly,' Mr. Under-Sheriff Dane Lee?"

Ut-oh! This is one of the traps that women set that no matter what you say, it comes out of your mouth sounding stupid and foolish and almost certainly like a lie. Been my experience to do a fade out and change the subject in tactical situations such as this. As I turned up the radio as a diversion tactic, country musician David Allan Coe's music and lyrics to his song "Longhaired Redneck" filled the interior of the Blazer.

Country deejays knows that I'm an outlaw,
They'd never come to see me in this dive.

My musical distraction was not working as the tension filled the air, and Nickey was still looking at me for an answer. With nowhere to hide, I looked at the woman I loved and just the vision of her sitting there set my blood on fire with desire. I had never met a woman like her before. She was thirty-one and of Mexican and Jewish descent; she was intelligent; and she had a great sense of humor; and she has those eyes! Her eyes were brown with a hint of blue, which was just icing on the cake as they complemented her natural beauty. Her hair was shoulder length and midnight black on her 5'8" slender frame, and I loved to hold her hair in my hand right before we would go to sleep. When awake, it was difficult not to stare as she walked away because her butt was a total class act all by itself. She was by far the most beautiful woman I had ever met, and it made me proud that she saw fit to spend her time with me. Mi Vida was her nickname that her mom had given her back home in Phoenix, Arizona, which meant "my life" in Spanish. Thinking of Nickey as Mi Vida seemed rather fitting for me, and Nickey had become "my life." She had moved here to Grand County about three years ago, and we met at work. Her first and middle names are Nickey and Lynn, and I called her both Nickey and Nickey Lynn. All of that flashed through my mind before I spoke, "Mi Vida, you are the only one that makes my heart race."

Nickey's half smile went full face as she responded to what I had said. Then her smile faded as she gingerly touched the six-inch scar on the right side of her face that Samael Amos had inflicted on her last year not more than a half mile from this very spot. Amos, a Rocky Mountain National Park Ranger psychopath, had killed deputy Gene Sanford and had left Nickey for dead after slicing her face and stabbing her several times. It truly was a miracle she had lived through the ordeal. Reaching out, I pressed gently on her forefinger touching the scar and said with all the love that I could muster for this woman, "This Mi Vida means nothing." Moving my hand slowly until I had the palm of my hand pressing in the center between her breasts where I could feel her heartbeat, I said, "This means everything; our hearts are joined as one. You are my life, Nickey Lynn!"

Nickey's eyes looked into mine, and she saw that all that I had said was the truth. She was forever mine, and I was forever hers. The beautiful moment we were now sharing was cut short by Yvonne, the Grand County Sheriff dispatcher. The police band radio cracked loudly as Yvonne said, "All units, be advised of a possible bank robbery in process. A silent alarm has been activated at the Grand Mountain Bank branch in Grand Lake."

Turning off the AM/FM radio, I looked at Nickey and saw the confusion that flooded her face. She slowly opened the door and stepped out of the Blazer and drew her sidearm. Grabbing the black radio mic of the police band radio, I keyed it and said, "Dispatch, could you repeat location of possible bank robbery."

The radio was silent for several seconds then crackled before Yvonne spoke again, "Silent alarm activated at Grand Mountain Bank, 902 Grand Avenue in Grand Lake."

Keying the mic once again, "Be advised that Nickey and I are on-site. Repeat, Nickey and I are on site."

Looking at Nickey, I shrugged my shoulders as we both looked around the street; it was just like any other time full of peaceful tourists going from shop to shop hauling bags of overpriced doodads that are found in these small mountain getaways. Before stepping out of the Blazer, I reached behind the seat and grabbed the Ruger Mini-14 rifle and slid it out of its scabbard. Nickey was still standing with the Blazer's passenger door open and said, "What are you thinking, Dane?"

Still not seeing anything that would show a bank robbery was taking place, I told Nickey, "Thinking it is probably a false alarm, but just in case, I need you to cover me as I approach the front door."

Using the open door of the Blazer as a shield, Nickey leveled her Ruger Security-Six double-action revolver chambered for a 38 round at the glass of the front door of the bank. Using the shoulder sling attached to the Ruger Mini-14 rifle, I draped it over my shoulder and let it ride on my back as I palmed my 357 3-screw Ruger Blackhawk from my service holster. Just as I was about to step out from behind the driver's side open door of the Blazer, the front door of the bank was slung so hard that the glass shattered as it slammed into the wall next to the door.

A man roughly six feet tall wearing a ski mask, camouflage fatigues, a military vest holding ten to twelve loaded magazines stepped through the door and leveled an Israeli Uzi submachine gun in our direction and fired off an entire magazine. The first volley took out the windshield and both doors of the Blazer's windows during the assault. Everything had happened so fast that neither Nickey nor I could return fire in the initial assault because of exploding glass and heavy thumps as the bullets thankfully did not penetrate the Chevy's heavy metal doors. Once the gunman finished the entire clip and was reloading, it gave Nickey and me an opening to return fire. At the same time, Nickey and I let loose with our service weapons which drove the ski-masked gunman back through the front door.

With sweat now streaking down my face, I reloaded as I yelled, "Nickey are you hit?"

I could hear Nickey breathing heavy with exertion as she reloaded as well and in a voice calmer than mine, "No, no I am fine. What the hell is that he is shooting at us with?"

Reaching inside the Blazer, I grabbed the mic of the police radio and stretched the black coiled cord to its max as I keyed the transmit button. "Be advised, shots fired, shots fired, gunman inside the Grand Mountain Bank is heavily armed with what looks like an Uzi submachine gun. Gunman has multiple magazines of ammo strapped to his chest."

The radio fell silent, and I was wondering if it had been damaged in the burst of machine gun fire. Seconds later it crackled to life with the voice of my boss Grand County Sheriff Tom Walker. "Dane, be advised two other units and I are in route. The highway patrol is responding as well. How many suspects?"

Looking through the interior of the Blazer, I could see Nickey on the other side, and she had already taken up a defensive position and had her service pistol at ready. Damn, I was proud of this woman. Keying the mic, I answered the Sheriff's question. "Be advised, only one assailant seen, possibly more inside the bank. More than likely bad guy has hostages."

With nothing more to say, I let go of the mic, and the black coil cord hurled the mic so hard there was a large "plunk" when it slammed into the dash. Speaking calmly, but loudly enough so there would be no misunderstanding, "Nickey we are outgunned and need to retreat across the street until the cavalry is here. I will cover you as you stay low and move as fast as your little legs will take you across the street. Set up behind the green Ford F-250.

Once in position, you give me cover fire as I retreat to your position. Do you understand?"

Nickey spoke with authority in the mounting tension of the moment. "Got it Dane! Don't be a hero and get all shot up! You still haven't answered my question about Kimberly!"

After I holstered my 357, Nickey's reply - even in the heat of battle - made me chuckle. Taking my Mini-14 rifle and not wanting to hit any innocents that may be in the bank, I aimed just above the broken front door. Once in position I looked to my right straight at Nickey Lynn through the interior of the shot-to-hell Blazer, and she nodded her head "yes" showing she was ready. Pulling the trigger as fast as it was possible, I unloaded the full magazine of twenty of the Mini-14 into the barn wood just above the front door as a diversionary tactic as Nickey made it safely across the street.

With the now empty Ruger rifle, I laid it on the front seat of the Blazer. Looking across the street, I could see Nickey staged up behind the green Ford F-250. Once again, she nodded her head "yes" telling me she was ready. Palming my 357, I made ready for my dash across the street. Nodding my head in a silent "yes," I showed to Nickey I was ready. Nickey, in a more disciplined manner, unloaded her Security Six into the wall just above the front door, as I had done.

Once safely across the street, I took up the defensive position as Nickey reloaded her pistol. Once her pistol was ready, she moved closer next to me as we both leveled our service weapons at the front door of the Grand Mountain Bank.

Looking side to side and up and down Grand Avenue, I could see the tourists and citizens had taken cover during the initial onslaught aimed at Nickey and me. I was thankful that it did not seem anyone had caught a stray bullet or ricochet. Hopefully, no one inside the bank had been harmed as well.

Finally, in the distance, I could hear the sirens of the Highway Patrol and the Grand County Sheriff Blazers in route to our position. Help was on the way.

Just as that last thought crossed my mind, a strange sound could be heard above the police sirens in the distance, "chuff, chuff, and chuff." Both Nickey and I were confused as to what the sound could be. Nickey saw it before I did as she pointed to the west down Grand Avenue. The whirring blades of a small bright red helicopter had generated the "chuff" that was now headed in our direction.

The two-seater helicopter was an Enstrom F-28C, fitted with an upgraded engine with turbocharger and a two piece windscreen. F-28C a small, light piston engine powered helicopter was produced by the Enstrom Helicopter Corporation.

Once I saw the helicopter, I realized who the bank robbers were and what was really going on. Nickey said, "I didn't know the Highway Patrol could dispatch a helicopter so fast."

Looking at Nickey Lynn, I shook my head "no," and said, "It is not the highway patrol, hell it isn't even any of the good guys. This bank robbery and that helicopter are the work of the Posse Comitatus. Or at least the more radical and militant arm of the Posse Comitatus. They call themselves the Insurgence."

Now knowing what we were truly facing, I told Nickey, "Get ready. The guy in the bank will try to use the helicopter to escape in. It was their plan all along and we just stumbled into the beginning of it."

Once the helicopter touched down on Grand Avenue, the gunman with a green army rucksack strapped onto his back, which I presumed had the bank's money in it, stepped onto the front boardwalk. The ski-masked gunman was holding on tightly to a young blonde-headed woman in front of him. He was using the girl as a human shield so we would not fire on him. The distance was too great to risk any shots with pistols. There was absolutely nothing we could do about it. About half-way to the helicopter, the gunman stopped and looked across the street directly in my eyes and leveled his Uzi in our direction and started spraying bullets. The Ford F-250, just like my Blazer, took all the gunman offered as once again we were peppered with the wreckage of shattered auto glass as all the windows were shot out in the attack. The heavy metal of the side of the truck stopped all the bullets as he unloaded another magazine in our direction. Once he was done with that magazine, he popped the magazine out and reloaded a fresh clip. Reloaded, he shoved the young girl to the ground and starting in again shooting a full magazine at Nickey and me. All we could do was hunker down and listen to the constant thumping as the bullets embedded into the side of the Ford pickup.

Whirring blades and the sound of "chuff, chuff" increased as the Enstrom F-28C gained altitude. By the time the gunman had quit shooting at us and we could peek above the bed of the shot-up Ford pickup, the helicopter; the pilot; and the bank robber were streaking over the top of the evergreens at full throttle headed north toward Rocky Mountain National Park.

CHAPTER 2

Once the Enstrom F-28C helicopter had cleared Grand Avenue and the surrounding trees to the north, Nickey and I quickly moved across the street. Nickey moved toward the young blonde-headed woman who had been used as a human shield, and I went directly up the wooden steps with my service pistol at ready. Flattening against the barn wood sided wall next to the broken glass front door, I yelled out, "Grand County Sheriff's Department, are there any more assailants in the building?"

A voice that I knew spoke loud and clear. Hope Jones, the long-time teller at this branch of Grand Mountain Bank, said, "Only that one asshole Dane; come on in, just don't shoot anyone."

*

For the rest of the day, Grand Lake, Colorado was not the normal mountain getaway people imagined. Every Grand County deputy and numerous state patrol officers had been called in and since Tom Walker the Grand County Sheriff reckoned that "The

Insurgence" could possibly be involved, there now were agents from the Denver office of the FBI in route to our location.

Since Nickey and I were the only ones that had exchanged gunfire with the bank robber, we had been isolated and separated from the rest of the law enforcement. And now we were sitting on a bench in front of the Lariat Saloon waiting to be interviewed by the Federal Bureau of Investigation. Even though Grand Avenue was awash with red and blue flashing lights of all the police cars, the jukebox was playing inside the Lariat to those enjoying a vacation dinner and beer. The music was loud, and the next song that played made Nickey and me look at each other with wide eyes, and then we started to laugh. Eric Clapton's version of Bob Marley's song "I Shot the Sheriff" came blaring out into the street.

I shot the sheriff,
But I did not shoot the deputy.

After the laughter, Nickey's smile faded slowly and had been replaced by a look of sadness and anxiety. She inched closer to me on the bench, and I wrapped my right arm over her as she looked me in the eyes and said, "Dane, I was so frightened. I thought we both would die."

The love of my life was now starting to feel the impact of how close we both came to dying here on the streets of Grand Lake. The adrenaline rush of the gun battle was starting to wear off both of us, and the longer we sat here, the more exhausted we would become. At that moment when confronted with a deadly adversary, we were prepared because we had been trained to react without emotions, and that is exactly what we had done - we fought the bank robber with training and knowledge. In that moment, no feelings were involved. We developed our killer instinct as they had taught us to do, and it took over like it was meant to be. Obviously, our training and a lot of luck saved our lives. I could feel Nickey's heartbeat as she pressed up against me, and it reminded me how much I loved this woman. Knowing she needed reassurance from me as much as I needed it from her, I pulled her a tad tighter and whispered, "Mi Vida, we did it exactly right. We fought and stood our ground even when we were outgunned. We survived to live another day. I was so proud of you and the warrior spirit you showed today. I cannot think of another man or woman I would want by my side when my life, our lives, are held in the balance of our actions."

Nickey moved her chin upward as an invitation, and I took it and I kissed her with all the heartfelt love I had for her. In just over a year, she had been through more trauma than most police officers do in a lifetime of wearing a badge. She had almost been killed and her face scarred for life by Samael Amos last year and now this - a shoot-out with what I am sure was the radical militant group the Insurgence that sprang from the ranks of the less radical Posse Comitatus. As my great grandfather Matt Lee, the famous mountain man would have said, "She is one to ride the river with." Nickey still holding me and looking in my eyes smiled and replied, "Thank you Dane, not sure what I would do without my half mountain man, half Ute Indian, all rolled into a very handsome man that somehow finds me attractive."

When Nickey was speaking to me, she instinctively reached up and touched the six-inch knife scar that Samael Amos had inflicted on her face. Even when Nickey wasn't thinking about the disfigurement, the pain of the mutilation was always there in her subconscious and from time to time she would touch the knife scar. Trying to break all the seriousness for a minute, I chuckled and said, "Well, Mrs. Nickey Lynn Chavez Lee, there is nothing in this world that would take your half-breed husband away from you. Except maybe that red-headed Kimberly."

Nickey's face lit up with that smile I loved so much, and she play slapped me while she was starting to laugh.

For the next several minutes, we watched all the activity on Grand Avenue with our brothers in arms going back and forth in their investigation of the bank robbery. In the surreal setting in this mountain getaway, we listened to the music coming from the jukebox inside the Lariat Saloon. Nickey squeezed my hand lovingly when the Elton John and Kiki Dee song "Don't Go Breaking My Heart" reached out past the open saloon doors.

Right from the start,
I gave you my heart.

The next song that played on the jukebox was Grand County's own Laney McKay. The local blonde-headed twenty-two year old girl had hit the big time after she moved to Nashville, Tennessee and currently had the billboard number one country song "Long Days, Lonely Nights." Both Nickey and I loved this song, and we were more than happy to have a local celebrity who was both kind-hearted and talented. Laney was younger than Nickey and I, but we knew her from attending the local high school football games. The purple pride "Panthers" were from Middle Park High School in Granby. Since I was an alumnus of the school and had played football for the Panthers, we attended every game that we could and had gotten to know Laney who even after graduation tried to make each home game. If the Sky-Hi News, the local Grand County newspaper out of Winter Park, was correct it would seem that Laney was returning home soon for a charity concert to help raise much needed money for the Grand County school system. It felt good to have her giving back to the community she grew up in. After Laney's number one song finished, it started over once again. It would seem that Laney McKay had a fan with a pocket full of quarters for the jukebox in the Lariat Saloon.

Long Days, Lonely Nights

Can't count the miles
Or the months of emptiness
Shed a million tears
I recall the sound of your voice
When you told me goodbye
I said darlin', you're makin' a big mistake
As you walked out the door
Falling apart
Is what I do best
Counting the miles

WHEN THE SONG VANISHES

Of all the emptiness
Millions of tears
That I have shed
With the voices of memories
Singing in my head

Falling apart is what I do best
Counting the scars of all my broken mess
The pain and the doubt and the loneliness
Falling apart is what I do best

Darling
It's a mistake
Walking out the door
Please don't take
Our love
And shake it
To the core
It will be the long days
And the lonely nights
And it will be us
No more
Please don't take our love
Walking out the door

Falling apart is what I do best
Counting the scars of all my broken mess
The pain and the doubt and the loneliness
Falling apart is what I do best

Night had settled in as Laney's song had faded in the background and the smell of the pine trees was wafting on a northern breeze that gently rolled across Grand Lake when two ebony 1976 Cadillac Fleetwood Brougham sedans rolled into the village. It would seem that the Federal Bureau of Investigation was now on site.

Nickey chuckled as she stated the obvious, "Those Feds know how to travel in style. What do those Cadillacs get – eight to nine miles to the gallon?"

Smiling, I replied, "If they get that. I'm sure it would have cost both of our paychecks just to drive those monstrosities the two and a half hours from Denver over Berthoud Pass."

After the sedans came to a stop almost in front of us, six men, all dressed identically with black ties over white button-down shirts and black suits, got out of the cars. The tallest man with short gray hair had a little more strut when he walked, and I assumed this one to be the boss. Sheriff Walker had made his way over and spoke with the one I thought was the boss and after about fifteen minutes, the Sheriff and the FBI agent turned our way and started walking toward us.

Nickey and I both stood as they walked up the wooden steps to the boardwalk in front of the saloon. Sheriff Walker introduced us, "Dane and Nickey, this is the lead investigator for the FBI Ken Ekross from the Denver office."

CHAPTER 3

Ken Ekross was about 6'1" and was built like a prizefighter
looking to be about 185 pounds. He was probably in his late fifties
with gray hair and no facial hair. I had no doubt that the lead
investigator was a no-nonsense man and was able to take care of
himself in a fistfight if it came down to it. His eyes showed the
man's intelligence and being how he was employed as a lead
investigator by the FBI, he had to be well disciplined. It would
seem Mr. Ekross didn't have or take time for pleasantries and got
straight to the point. "I know both of you from the news last year
regarding the attack on Nickey and subsequent manhunt for
Samael Amos in Rocky Mountain National Park. I have read your
files on the drive up here from Denver and your boss here gives
you both accolades for being top officers of the law. I am not here
to rake you over the coals of what could or should have been done
here today because I know you did the best you could do given the
circumstances. It is the FBI's and my belief that we are dealing
with the Insurgence. The helicopter you saw that was used in the
bank hold-up and escape matches the description of a helicopter
stolen at Centennial Airport in Arapahoe County less than a week
ago. The helicopter and the lone bank robber match the method of

operation of the radical militant group. My guess is they came, they stole, and they are long gone from your jurisdiction. Unless you have something to add to the reports that you have already written, you are free to resume your duties as the Sheriff sees fit."

Nothing like being dismissed in an orderly fashion, but I was actually okay with it. Nickey, on the other hand, was a bit peeved and was needing more information on what happened today. With the sound of annoyance in her voice, Nickey said, "Ken, may I call you Ken? You and your 'dress a likes' are here for five minutes and you swat us away like a couple of pesky flies. We might be just a bunch of mountain hillbillies to you city folks but believe it or not, we care about this community that we have sworn to protect. I know you think your time is more valuable than ours and I might be a tad slow in the uptake, but I have no idea who in the hell just robbed this bank and tried to kill Undersheriff Lee and myself. So, Ken, you can suck it up and spend a few more minutes of your freakin' time informing us what the Feds know so we hillbillies can protect our community better."

Federal agent in charge Ekross' eyes and demeanor showed that he was not accustomed to being spoken to in such a manner. Sheriff Tom Walker was standing behind Ekross with a smile as big as all the outdoors. I was positive my grin matched his. Nickey had moved in closer to Ekross and was looking him in the eye as if challenging him to dismiss her once again. It was like the typical western showdown in a John Wayne or Clint Eastwood movie - like this town is not big enough for the both of us type of showdown. Then the unexpected happened and the hard-nosed federal agent Ekross chuckled as he replied, "My apologies Deputy Chavez."

Nickey snarled a little when she cut off Ekross and said, "Deputy Lee, Ken; my name is Deputy Lee."

My guess was Ken's reports on Nickey and me were not as up to date as they led him to believe. He stood silent for a few seconds before swinging his forefinger back and forth in between Nickey and me before speaking. "You two are married? Now that is interesting."

Nickey still in a half-snarl, "Yes Ken, the two of us are married and don't even go there. All I want is a situational update on what my husband and I faced today and may face in the future."

Ken's demeanor softened, and he chuckled once again knowing he met his match today. "Understood, Deputy Lee."

Ken pointed to the bench Nickey and I had been sitting on earlier and said, "You might want to sit down; this might take more than a few minutes. There was a wooden stool next to the bench and Ken pulled it up in front of the bench and looked not at me, but at Nickey and said, "May I?"

Nickey said in a more pleasant and friendly tone, "Yes, of course Ken."

Sheriff Walker was still all grins and with a truce in effect between Nickey and Ken and not needing an update since he already knew who we were dealing with, he stepped down off the boardwalk and headed across the street to check on how the investigative team was doing. Once we were all seated, Ken started in on the update, "Guessing the first place to start is the beginning. Posse Comitatus is a legal term and became United States federal law in 1878 by President Rutherford B. Hayes. The purpose of the act - in concert with the Insurrection Act of 1807 - is to limit the powers of the federal government in using federal military personnel to enforce domestic policies within the United States. The whole idea was to limit the use of the military to enforce civilian law."

Most of this I already knew, but it was all new and interesting history for Nickey. Nickey said, "I am a little confused. That all sounds very American and like the right thing to do. Not following how this involves a bank robbery in Grand Lake."

Ken, who now took on the role of professor that had found a willing student, seemed almost pleased to pass along this information as he continued, "The Posse Comitatus Act is about American as it gets. And as it is written, it is the right thing to do. But some folks look at the law sideways and interpret it to fit their own agenda. In the last fifteen years, an organization has sprung up around Dodge City, Kansas of some militant farmers calling themselves the 'Posse Comitatus.' They have taken a good law as their name of their group and twisted the true meaning of the purpose of the law. Even though their politics and mine are aligned, they have taken it to the far-right extreme. They are anti-government and conspiracy minded. They believe the government has overstepped and has attacked their social and political rights. They have their own radio station in Dodge City, and they use it as a platform to spread their agenda through the airways. They avoid paying taxes and most of the 'Posse' members practice survival apocalypse end of the world type lives. They are well-stocked, well-armed and feel ready to join into the overthrow of the United States government if needed. The FBI keeps tabs on this group, but until a year ago the only illegal activity that some members had done was some tax evasion. Those cases are being handled in the courts by the Internal Revenue Service."

Nickey was riveted as Ken spoke about the Posse Comitatus. I had already known about their existence but had learned more in the last few minutes from the FBI agent than I could have ever learned from the Denver Post or Rocky Mountain News - the two rival newspapers in Denver. While Nickey was processing all the information she had just learned, I asked what was begging to be asked, "Ken, you said 'until a year ago.' What happened a year ago?"

Ken cleared his voice and breathed deeply before starting in again. "There was a falling out in the Posse's leadership. Six of the younger members that had recently finished their tours in Vietnam had become dissatisfied in the non-aggressive direction that the Posse was moving. These six members are all highly trained individuals from the Special Forces with over 100 combat missions among them. As you may have gathered, at least one is a helicopter pilot that flew in over thirty combat missions in Vietnam and Cambodia. These six want to overthrow the government...now! Since the Posse in their minds was useless in the endeavor to do so, the six split off and formed what we now know as 'The Insurgence.' To fund their overthrow, they have resorted to robbing banks. They execute each bank robbery with clockwork military planning and organization. Their current method of operations is just exactly what you saw today. They steal a helicopter and then they pick a small-town bank like the one here in Grand Lake. The law enforcement is spread thinly so they expect little or no resistance. That changed today when you both confronted them here during the robbery. Although no one has been killed during their robberies that does not mean these guys are against it. If confronted, they will kill as both of you found out today during your gun battle with the bank robber. The Insurgence see themselves as patriots, but in reality, they are nothing more than just common criminals. All six men are deadly, cunning, and lethal, and next week they will be added to the FBI's most wanted list. Good news for Grand County is you have probably seen the last of the Insurgence."

CHAPTER 4

The following week, after the bank robbery in Grand Lake, was full of meetings with various law enforcement agencies that were helping the FBI with their investigation. By helping, I mean the Grand County Sheriff's Department ran crowd control for the press from Denver and all the local onlookers that flocked to Grand Lake. It would seem the Grand Mountain bank robbery was the biggest newsworthy event to happen in Grand County since the man hunt for Samael Amos last year. That was about to change though as Laney McKay had now scheduled her charity event concert in Grand Lake on Labor Day Weekend. Labor Day was Monday the fifth of September; Laney's concert would be on Sunday the fourth starting at nine p.m.

The production company for Laney McKay had already started setting up a huge stage covered by an even larger canvas awning in Town Square Park in between Pitkin St. and Garfield St. Nickey and I were just happy; since we had to work crowd control at the concert, we didn't have to pony up the ten dollars per ticket to see our friend.

On Thursday before Labor Day weekend, I woke up at three a.m. in a cold sweat. I had not had a dream of my grandfather Matt Lee since the death of Samael Amos. I closed my eyes and tried to recall the details of the dream, for I knew my grandfather was trying to tell me something, something important, something that could mean life or death. Wiping the sweat from my brow, I concentrated on the dream. *On a wilderness trail Nickey was running ahead of me, and ahead of her were another woman and a man running in the same direction. I knew it was early autumn from the sweet smell of decaying leaves. Although the trail we were running on felt familiar, I could not place the exact location in my mind except that I knew it to be in Rocky Mountain National Park. Running a little faster, I caught up with Nickey and I could see the exertion of running for our lives in the redness of her face and the deep breaths she was taking. Nodding in a silent command for her and the others to keep moving forward, I stopped to face what was behind us. The look of worry of one that loves you flooded her face, but she nodded and pushed on as I slowed my pace. Palming my weapon, I turned to face what was behind us. Nothing, nothing was there except a black crow. The crow landed on an evergreen right before me not ten feet away, and the crow's ebony black feathers glistened from the sunlight and the shadows as it jumped from limb to limb until it finally settled on a perch to watch me with intelligent eyes. From my Ute Indian heritage, I knew the crow was a powerful spirit, and they were all-knowing in the spirit world. My Ute ancestors believed the crow knew all the mysteries of life and death. Sometimes they would appear and point you to a certain path that your life should follow. Sometimes they would show themselves foretelling of an impending death. As I was pondering the meaning of this crow, I felt a new presence behind me. I slowly turned and there was a man sitting on a rock ten feet away whittling a piece of aspen wood with a large Bowie knife. He was older than I was by at least thirty years but still seemed to have the grace of one much younger. The apparition was my height and weight and he looked like me - just older with shoulder length hair white as snow. Although I had never seen a photograph of my grandfather since there was none, I knew this was he, for he had visited me many times before in my dreams - the famous mountain man Matt Lee and the greatest foe the Ute Indians had ever faced - the one they called "Ghost" for his uncanny ability to fade into the*

Rocky Mountains after battling his ancient enemy. Grandfather stopped his whittling and looked directly into my soul as he spoke with a commanding and deep voice, "Dane, the enemy is not the white warrior."

This dream, just like the ones before in my life, had more questions than answers. Why were we running? What were we running from? Who were the two other people with Nickey? Who was the white warrior? What was a white warrior? If the white warrior was not the enemy, who was the enemy? These dreams of my grandfather were part of the Lee clan legacy and always foretold of future events. What this one meant at this juncture I did not have a clue. All I know is I felt the sense of an ominous foreboding of something in the not-so-distant future, and this was the calm before the storm.

Matt Lee was my great, great, great grandfather and was a legend in mountain man history, known for his battles against his enemies. I believe he and my grandmother died in the 1880's. Grandfather buried my grandmother in the hidden valley called Redemption Valley on Boreas Pass. Soon after, grandfather died in a successful rescue attempt of the granddaughter of the famous Marshal Eric Robert, but that is another story altogether.

I could not go back to sleep as the dream with my grandfather kept filtering through my mind. At five a.m. I rolled over and watched Nickey sleep. It was a guilty pleasure I had watching her slumber. She always seemed so peaceful and so at peace at this time in the morning, and I could not even imagine loving another woman like I did Nickey. Nickey's peaceful sleep had just returned two months ago as the nightmares of her closeness to death seemed to fade. Reaching out, I gently gathered in a handful of her hair and brought it closer to me so I could smell her essence. As I had proven to myself in the death of Samael Amos, there was nothing I would not do for this woman. She was my world; she was *Mi Vida*.

Deciding to let Nickey sleep a little longer, I got up and stood in front of the mirror in our bathroom looking at my reflection. After splashing water on my face to refresh and clear the dreams in my head, I wondered what a woman like Nickey saw in a man like me. Even though women had always been attracted to me, I was thirty-two years old and never really thought of myself as handsome; I thought my face looked haggard for a man my age. I was 6'2'' and weighed 200 pounds, with strong and tight muscles that came natural to the Lee men. My hair was the color of coal and I had brown eyes. On a scale of one to ten, I thought I was maybe a six. Nickey thought differently, and that was all that really mattered. I worked out four days a week at the high school gym to keep in shape and spent most of my free time up in Rocky Mountain National Park mountain climbing and pushing my body and mind to the limit in my self-styled survival training. My dad was a mountain man through and through, just like his father and grandfathers all the way back to Matt Lee. It is in the Lee blood to be one with nature and to understand the wilderness of the Rocky Mountains. The men of Lee had known for generations you never conquer the mountains or the wild; you learn to rejoice in the solitude and all that is nature. With the Lee men, the Rocky Mountains are a part of us, and it is who we are; my dad and my grandfathers before believed living a life in the wilderness was the equal of churchgoing.

After cleaning up a bit, I walked back into our bedroom and Nickey was lying in bed awake and she had been watching me as I pondered. Smiling at me she said, "You seemed to be in deep thought, Mr. Lee. What were you contemplating?"
Sitting down on the edge of the bed and looking at her, knowing I could keep nothing from her I replied, "Had a grandfather dream last night."

The smile disappeared from her face as she processed what I had said because she knew in my dreams of my grandfather there would be something important for us to know. After about a minute she said, "Been a while since you had a dream of him. Did you understand the message he brought?"

Running the dream quickly through my head once more, I shook my head "no," and then replied, "Not yet, but give it time and I will. Probably should get up my love; we got a meeting with the FBI this morning at eight."

She glanced at our bedside alarm clock and smiled; then she pulled back the blanket revealing her nakedness and with an alluring smile said, "We got a little bit of time; crawl back in here and make your woman happy."

I never could say no to Nickey and now was not the time to start. As I gathered her into my arms I said, "We have time!"

CHAPTER 5

Nickey and I made it to our Grand County Sheriff's office in Hot Sulphur Springs just in time for the meeting with Ken Ekross of the FBI. As we walked into the small and old building at 670 Spring Street, the front door once again was stubborn and both Nickey and I had to grab it to muscle it open. Every time I came to work, it reminded me how ancient this building was. Not sure when it was built, but Hot Sulphur Springs had become a town in 1860 and was the oldest established town in Grand County. Although the building was timeworn, poorly laid out, and the heating inside was uneven with no air conditioning, I loved this building. It had a feeling of history and mystery of law enforcement from days gone by dating all the way back to the old west.

As we did every time we walked down the entrance hallway, we both touched the missing poster of my long-lost friend Micah Trask. As Nickey moved ahead of me toward the squad room, I stopped for a few seconds and quickly relived what I knew about my best friend's disappearance. I was the only one who knew the truth that Micah was long dead. Looking below Micah's missing poster was a wanted poster for Samael Amos, which was still pinned to the board. They had found Amos' remains in Rocky Mountain National Park. Once again, I was the only one who knew the truth on how Samael Amos had died. If not for me, Amos the serial killer may still be killing and spreading his evil across Grand County. I was with him when he died and was the orchestrator of his death. Nickey and Sheriff Tom Walker suspected the truth in both matters, but Samael Amos was a closed case now. Some Rocky Mountain frontier secrets are better left unsaid.

The squad room was hot, stuffy, and packed with Grand County Sheriff employees as Ken Ekross and his look-a-like sidekick took front and center. Ekross stood up, straightened his tie, and cleared his voice and began to speak, "Our investigation into the Grand Mountain Bank robbery is still ongoing. Having said that, the FBI has gathered all the evidence and interviewed all the witnesses here in Grand County that we could, so we will continue our investigation from our offices in Denver. We believe from the method of operation and the similar circumstances of the robbery that we are in fact dealing with the militant arm of the Posse Comitatus - the one calling themselves "The Insurgence." Our agents in Kansas have been visiting the homes of known Posse Comitatus and The Insurgence members in Lane, Ness, Finney, Hodgeman, and Ford counties. We could not locate six members of The Insurgence. As you can see, my assistant is now passing out flyers with those six missing members' names, photos, and a summary of their bios. Once you have read these, you will get a better feeling on how dangerous these men are. The good news for Grand County is that the FBI feels you have seen the last of these men. We are confident that they have moved on to apply their brand of criminal activity elsewhere."

Looking at the papers handed to me, I studied the bios of the men of The Insurgence.

Dan Minuex - the photo of Dan had been taken in what looked like a mop-up action in Vietnam. In the full body photo of Dan, he was wearing the typical tiger-striped jungle fatigues with a matching tiger-striped boonie-hat. He looked as you would expect of a soldier in combat, fit and trim. His face was hard and lean with piercing eyes. According to his bio, he was born in Lane County, Kansas, and by all accounts his upbringing was that of a typical farm kid. His grades were in the top ten percent of his class. After graduation he joined the military and showed enough aptitude to be given a slot in the Green Berets and had risen to the rank of Master Sergeant. He was a weapons specialist and served in Vietnam with the Fifth Special Forces Group, who had their headquarters in Nha Trang. He served three tours in Vietnam. He was highly decorated and was honorably discharged. His age now was Thirty-two years old. I had a feeling it was Dan Minuex who was the lone bank robber Nickey and I had confronted at Grand Mountain Bank.

Mitch Minuex - the photo of Mitch was that of a smiling, slender man sitting in a helicopter with his helmet off. Mitch was the younger brother of Dan with the same upbringing except after graduation he became a member of Air Cavalry Division and became a helicopter combat pilot of the well-known First Squadron/Ninth Cavalry. Mitch also served three tours in Vietnam. The First Squadron, Ninth Cavalry took part in such pivotal battles as the Ia Drang Valley, Khe Sahn, Binh Dinh, and Quang Tri. He was highly decorated and was honorably discharged. He was a born and raised American hero, just like his older brother. His age now was thirty years old. Mitch obviously was the one flying the helicopter during the escape after the bank robbery.

Boyd Thomas - the photo of Boyd was also a full body photo taken in the jungles of Vietnam. He looked strong and fit and was wearing the typical tiger-striped jungle fatigues with a matching tiger-striped boonie-hat. Boyd was the same age of the older Minuex brother and was also from Lane County, Kansas. It appears he was a good friend in high school with both of the Minuex brothers and had enlisted into the military on the same day as Dan Minuex. He also was given a slot in the Green Berets and served in the Fifth Special Forces Group, who had their headquarters in Nha Trang. He had risen to the rank of Sergeant First Class. His specialty was communications and oversaw the sophisticated communications equipment of any team they assigned him to. He was highly decorated and was honorably discharged. He was now thirty-two years of age.

Bob Jonasen - the photo of Bob was full body and showed another fit soldier wearing the battle dress of a Seventy-Fifth Infantry Regiment (Ranger) and was part of the Long Range Reconnaissance Patrol. They composed these Ranger companies of small, heavily armed with long range reconnaissance teams that patrolled deep in enemy-held territory. They attached each independent company to a division or separate brigade and acted as the eyes and ears of those units. Rangers collected intelligence; discovered enemy troop locations; surveilled trails and enemy hot spots; directed artillery and air strikes; did bombing damage assessment; and performed ambushes and sniper attacks. Jonasen was known as an expert marksman and sniper. Bob was born in South Dakota but raised in Ness County, Kansas, and grew up working in his father's grocery store in Ness City. After finishing high school, he also joined the military and became an Army Ranger and rose to the rank of Sergeant First Class. He served two tours in Vietnam. He was highly decorated and was honorably discharged. He was now thirty-one years of age.

Clarence O'Brien – He was a Marine and his photo was taken according to the description at the bottom of the photo during Operation Pursuit, initiated in mid-February 1968 by the First Marine Division to search for enemy rocket caches in the mountains west of Da Nang. Clarence looked worn and haggard in the photo. He was a medic and in the photo was attending to several wounded soldiers. Clarence served two tours in Vietnam. He was highly decorated and was honorably discharged. Clarence was from Lane County, Kansas. His father was the manager of the grain elevator in Healy, Kansas. After high school, he joined the military. He was now thirty-one years old.

Gary Lewis - His photo was his graduation photo from Dighton High School in Lane County, Kansas. He grew up helping his father in their auto repair garage in Dighton. Gary joined the military after high school and showed enough aptitude to be given a slot in the Green Berets and had risen to the rank of Master

Sergeant. He was a weapons specialist and served in Vietnam with the Fifth Special Forces Group, the same group as Dan Minuex and Boyd Thomas. He also served two tours in country. He was highly decorated and was honorably discharged. His age now was thirty-three years old.

I read each bio of each man twice and felt the power of the men that had been described. All six grew up with a sense of patriotism for their country. It would also seem that they all to a man had come from pretty much normal Kansas childhoods in the heartland of America. I wonder where their patriotism had gotten twisted. The last page was an FBI profiler that tried to answer that question. "We believe that after their tours in Vietnam, these highly trained soldiers returned home and expected accolades for what they had seen as fighting back communism and doing their patriotic duty. When they returned home, there were no parades or pats on the backs, and they had been met at the airports and had been protested for their commitment to America after their involvement in the jungles of Vietnam. They were spit on, shunned, and called baby killers. Returning to western Kansas was also not as they expected. Many of their families and friends had become disillusioned with the United States government and they formed the organization 'Posse Comitatus.' They believed that the American government had lost their way and had become too liberal and was sliding into the clutches of socialism and communism. Posse Comitatus became anti-government and conspiracy minded. They believed the government had overstepped and had attacked their social and political rights. They avoided paying taxes and most of the 'Posse' members practiced survival apocalypse end of the world type lives. They protested the government by tractor convoys to Washington. They bought a radio station in Dodge City, Kansas, and used it for their anti-government platform. Those that were fresh from Vietnam were angry, which turned into rage as it was their belief that the Posse was not doing enough and needed to take up arms and overthrow the government now. These frustrated six ex-soldiers separated themselves from the original Posse movement and started their own movement called "The Insurgence" with their only mission to attack and overthrow the American government. They are well stocked, well-armed, well-trained, but poorly financed. It is the FBI's belief that the bank robberies are being done to help finance this government coup attempt. These men are to be considered armed, dangerous, and a threat to national security."

I read the bios of the six Insurgence members twice. After Nickey finished reading her copies, I reached out to her to hand me her FBI reports after she got done reading them. Once she handed them to me, her eyes meet mine, and I said, "Nickey my love, I believe we were very, very lucky to walk away from that bank hold-up with our lives. These guys it would seem do not mess around or make many mistakes."

Taking both sets of documents, I opened the top drawer of my desk and laid them on top and as I slid the drawer closed, I said, "Glad we are done with the Insurgence and never will have to deal with the likes of them again!"

CHAPTER 6

Following the departure of the FBI from Grand County, everyone in the Grand County Sheriff's office was now focused on the upcoming Laney McKay benefit concert in three days on September fourth. This was a big event that everyone here was looking forward to. The whole county and the state of Colorado were proud of their local girl making it big in the national spotlight for her musical talents.

The production company for Laney McKay had the huge, covered stage and an even larger canvas awning and sound system setup and completed. Town Square Park in Grand Lake between Pitkin Street and Garfield Street had been cordoned off with traffic cones, and we had two sheriff deputies already manning the streets to keep the cars out of the road making the paved road a dance floor for all those that wanted to dance. Nickey and I were both looking forward to working the concert crowd control for our friend Laney. Laney quietly arrived in Grand County, spent Friday and most of Saturday with her family, and had dinner with Nickey and me on Saturday night. Laney was still the same sweet and lovable Middle Park girl whom we had grown to love. It was an enjoyable night eating chicken enchiladas and getting caught up. Laney McKay was an inspiration to all who knew her because she truly had not forgotten where she came from and could be a poster child for small-town values. Nickey and I were looking forward to her concert tomorrow night.

After Laney left after supper, Nickey and I settled in for the night and watched Laverne & Shirley. Following the lives and comedy of Laverne DeFazio and Shirley Feeney was one of Nickey's favorite things to do, and I had to admit it was a guilty pleasure of mine as well. Nickey would tease me all the time that if anyone knew how much I enjoyed watching the show that someone was going to show up one day and take my "man card" away from me. Of course, this made us both laugh.

During the ABC Evening News with Harry Reasoner and Barbara Walters, there was no mention of the Grand Lake bank robbery, Posse Comitatus, or the Insurgence. They now focused the news on the upcoming nuclear-proliferation pact meetings that hopefully would lead to treaties curbing the spread of nuclear weapons. It would seem that the world had now forgotten all about Grand County and Colorado.

As we got ready for bed, Nickey was wearing her red lace panties and her tight half-shirt with no bra and while brushing her teeth would look over her shoulder at me with her suggestive and alluring look. This was an old trick of hers when she wanted some loving. Of course, I fell for it every time. Following her into the bathroom, I moved up close to her from behind and with one hand brought her in tight so she could feel me and the heat of my passion. Lifting her hair, I slowly started kissing her neck as she turned to face me. As always in these tender moments, Nickey became self-aware of the scar on her face and with no thought she touched it to hide the disfigurement. Looking in her eyes, I slowly moved her hand away from the scar. The scar meant nothing to me, other than it meant something to this woman I loved. Seeing the love I felt for her in my eyes, she temporarily forgot the scar as our lips met.

After Nickey and I were spent after making love, she fell asleep quickly. For me, all I could do was lay there watching the love of my life as she slept peacefully. In recent days a sense of foreboding settled in on me as if something was just beyond my eyesight - something was out of kilter, something bad. It was midnight before I could fall asleep.

Jolting awake, I breathed quickly and shallowly. I quickly glanced to the bedside clock, and it was 4:36 a.m. realizing I had only slept for four and a half hours, I recalled the dream that had woken me up. *We had been running for our lives. Nickey and the other two were still ahead of me on the trail that felt so familiar. I turned to face who or what was behind us as I held my pistol at ready. Once again, as in the recent dream, all that was behind me was a black crow sitting on an evergreen branch. The crow was the warning from my Ute Indian heritage, and I tried to decipher the meaning of its presence once again. I was concentrating so hard on the crow that I had not felt the presence of Grandfather Matt Lee until he touched my shoulder. I was startled when I turned to look at him as he mouthed the words once again, "Dane, the enemy is not the white warrior."*

Knowing it was no use trying to get back to sleep, I threw my legs over the edge of the bed and looked out into the darkness through the bedroom window. What was grandfather trying to tell me? Who was the white warrior? Who were the other two people running ahead of Nickey?

After pondering these questions once again to no new revelation, I got up and headed to the bathroom and splashed some cold water on my face. As I looked in the mirror, the reflection that was looking back at me seemed troubled. I was troubled because my gut instinct was turning me inside out. Something was on the horizon that threatens Nickey and me. I just didn't know what yet. After a quick breakfast of pop-tarts and Tang orange drink, Nickey and I headed to work down Highway 40 to the sheriff's department in Hot Sulphur Springs. During the eleven-mile trek, I slipped in "Wanted! The Outlaws" cassette and the song "My Heroes Have Always Been Cowboys" by Waylon Jennings. Our Sheriff's Chevy

Blazer was filled with Waylon's deep iconic voice as we moved on down the highway.

Sadly, in search of, but one step in back of
Themselves and their slow-movin' dreams

We made it to the squad room for our briefing at exactly 8:02 a.m. Our very good friend John Combs looked at his watch, smiled and then mouthed the words, "You both are late!" This prompted Nickey and I both at the same time to flip him the bird, which made all three of us break into smiles.

Sheriff Walker gave us our work assignments and because the sheriff knew of Nickey's and my relationship to Laney McKay, he assigned us to be out front and center stage at Laney's concert tonight. We, along with John Combs, would prevent anyone that maybe had a little too much to drink from climbing on the stage to join the band. This concert was in Grand Lake, Colorado and we really did not expect too much trouble with all the tourists that would be in town tonight.

The rest of the day flew by quickly, and I was thankful we had packed some lunches and snacks for the day since we never had the time to have a sit-down meal. The Village of Grand Lake was overflowing with Laney McKay fans, and it seemed this concert and the charitable proceeds would be a wonderful addition for some much-needed cash into the school system. Nickey, John, and I were stationed in front of the stage, and we were having a good time. The other deputies were monitoring traffic and such. Everyone here was just looking to see and hear Laney, and the entire crowd seemed to be of the peaceful nature.

The day and now the night had turned out to have beautiful weather for the concert. The day had been in the upper 70's with sunshine and not a cloud in the sky. The night was just chilled enough that everyone had to wear light jackets, but other than that, the weather stayed cooperative as Grand County's own Laney McKay took the stage at 9:10 p.m. The crowd all hooted and hollered good-naturedly as they welcomed home Middle Park's most famous daughter.

Laney was all smiles as she started off with the song "Different Drum" that Linda Ronstadt had made famous.

You and I travel to the beat of a different drum
Ah, can't you tell by the way I run
Ever'time you make eyes at me?

It was during the second song of the evening, which was a Laney's original song called "Dark Nights," when I glimpsed Rod Edwards moving up to the stage. I knew Edwards, and he had a reputation as a troublemaker. Edwards moved through the crowd until he was standing just below, but directly in front of Laney. Not trusting him, I kept an eye on him.

Nickey followed my gaze and saw who I was looking at and said, "That Edwards kid gives me the creeps. He never smiles, and he seems to appear out of nowhere sometimes. He is like a ghost - he is not there, then he is there. Just weird! So, what is his story?" Laney seemed to enjoy the spotlight as she moved and danced across the stage singing one song after another to the crowd's obvious delight.

Rod Edwards was a full blooded Cheyenne Indian with long black hair to the middle of his back. In the long-forgotten past, his ancestors and my ancestors the Ute's were enemies at one time or another. Edwards was twenty-five years old, and his build was on a sturdy and muscular frame. He was 5'10" tall and probably weighed in around 185 pounds. Tonight, he was wearing a white t-shirt, a jean jacket, Levi's, and cowboy boots. Turning to look at Nickey and then back toward Rod, I pulled her in close so she could hear me above the crowd and answered her question, "His family ancestor stories are woven throughout Grand County history even way before Colorado was even a state. The men in his family are the last of the Dog Men, or as some historians call them

35

Cheyenne Dog Soldiers. They are, or were anyway, the elite Cheyenne warriors. His Cheyenne name is Ho'nehenotaxe, which translates into Soldier Wolf. He dropped out of high school and as soon as he could, he joined the military. He completed boot camp and was even selected for Special Forces training. Something happened while he was in Special Forces training and they gave him a military deferment at the 'Convenience of the Government' and kicked him out. What that incident was that gave him the deferment I never heard. He just showed back up here about a year after joining. He has been in a few bar fights here and there, and I even arrested him once for assault. The guy he beat up severely ended up in Saint Joseph's Hospital down in Denver for a couple of weeks. I drove to Denver to get the victim's statement, and he was so scared of Edwards he dropped all the charges and we had to let Edwards go. I saw him fight once, and he never loses control; he has a warrior mentality."

Nickey listened carefully and then said, "What is a Dog Man, or Dog Soldier, or whatever you called it?"

Nickey was still standing close, and I had to speak a little louder because of the crowd and Laney singing as I told her what I knew. "Every culture needs its heroes. Cheyenne Dog Soldiers were the Cheyenne nation's heroes. The Cheyenne ranged from Montana to Oklahoma to Colorado, to name a few places. Way back when the Cheyenne people had established the tradition of military societies, one of these societies was a sacred fraternity of men of the tribe known as the Dog Soldiers. They would become the most feared defenders of the Cheyenne people. Dog Soldiers were the bravest of the brave, and that meant their war bonnets could be especially elaborate. The most elite of the Dog Soldiers, the absolute best of the best, didn't just have war bonnets or sacred weapons - they also carried a length of rope. Now, these weren't any old pieces of rope found around camp. These tough pieces of rawhide, called dog ropes, were both a mark of honor and a promise made by the warrior to fight to the very end. The idea was that, during battle, someone carrying the dog rope would pin one end to the ground and fix the other end to themselves. That warrior would then fight within the small radius of the rope, showing that he was so utterly dedicated to battle that he would literally stand his ground to the death. The only way to be released from the dog rope was to be victorious in battle, unpinned by a higher-ranking warrior, or death. That is the heritage of Rod Edwards - alias "Soldier Wolf." The Cheyenne nation takes the standing of the Dog Soldiers seriously even today."

Nickey sort of chuckled with wide eyes and said, "That is what I was saying...he is just weird."

Laughing out loud, I said, "That is it in a nutshell... just weird!" My eyes drifted back to Soldier Wolf as he stood there looking at Laney McKay with intensity, and my own Ute Indian heritage was speaking deep down inside of me. My gut instinct and the recent dreams of grandfather walked hand in hand. Something ominous was going to happen soon.

CHAPTER 7

It was the seventh song of the night when Laney finally sang her recent number one hit "Long Days, Lonely Nights." And with the voice of an angel, she started singing her haunting ballad of lost love.

Falling apart is what I do best
Counting the scars of all my broken mess
The pain and the doubt and the loneliness

The song, Laney singing it, and this night became something magical as the entire crowd, including Nickey and I, sang "Long Days, Lonely Nights" along with Laney. It was really something amazing to hear and to see. It was a song that everyone at one time or another could relate to in their lives.

Just as the song ended, some local ranchers and rednecks made their way through the crowd to the front row and were standing next to Rod Edwards. All six of the ranchers were whooping and hollering and having a good time. Because of a previous experience in the Lariat saloon about six months ago, I knew that these boys, especially one named Kelly Reser and Edwards did not get along. Grabbing Nickey's hand so she would look at me, I nodded toward Edwards and the newcomers and said, "I think it is a good idea we meander over there and make our presence known."

Nickey and I were having trouble navigating through the crowd to get to Edwards and the others as the concert was still in full swing. It was taking longer than I hoped to get near Edwards and Reser just in front of Laney on stage.

It didn't take long for Reser and his redneck buddies to surround Edwards. Rod, just as I had seen before, was in total control of his emotions as he spoke with those that were now confronting him. The Cheyenne Dog Soldier showed no fear. The leader of the pack of local ranchers, Kelly Reser, was pointing a finger at Edwards as he stood on his tiptoes. I feared for the safety of the boy. Reser was a big kid at 6'3" and 250 pounds and twenty-four years old, but he was no match for Edwards. Kelly Reser was a blow-hard and a bully and was getting red in the face as the episode escalated to the point of no return. Just before Nickey and I reached the proximity of the young men, Reser spit a mouthful of chewing tobacco into Edwards' face. Edwards reacted far more quickly than anyone could have foreseen including me.

Edwards, with cat like moves, pulled a seven inch Kabar combat fighting knife from a leather sheath from under his shirt and within less than a second had Reser slammed to the ground with Edwards' right knee in his back and pulling Reser's head back. With his left hand clutching the young rancher's long dark hair, Edwards' right hand held the serrated Kabar knife to Reser's throat as the remaining rednecks stood in shock. They were motionless, waiting to see if Edwards would follow through and cut their friend's throat.

The crowd was slow to respond, but when they did, they silently moved backward into an ever-widening circle as they reacted to the confrontation. The tension was building and as it built, it was like time had stopped. Laney was still on stage, but the music had ceased as everyone including Laney and the band were now a witness to what was happening just before their eyes. Now that we had room to maneuver, Nickey and I moved in closer drawing our pistols and pointing them at Edwards. Edwards was pulling back hard on Reser's hair and with his knee in his back, Reser was having trouble just breathing. Out of the corner of my eye, I could see John Combs had made it and was also pointing his weapon at Edwards. Moving cautiously around so I could get into Edwards' line of sight, I said in a calm voice, "What exactly are you going to do now, Rod?"

"I haven't decided if I should cut his throat, take an ear, or take his scalp!"

Waiting until Edwards' eyes locked onto mine, "I need you to drop the Kabar and release the boy."

"And if I don't?"

This conversation was not going as I hoped it would. "It would force me to shoot you, Rod! Now, hear me and hear me good, I don't want to do that. It would make your mother very sad. I like your mom, and the last thing I would want to do is take her only boy's life!"

Edwards was not even breathing hard; it was as if he was taking a stroll on a Sunday afternoon. The kid had ice in his veins. Rod was silent for almost a full minute, and I feared Reser was going to black out from the way Edwards had him bent.

"Either way, you are going to arrest me!"

"That's not true, Rod; one way you get arrested, the other way you get dead. Choose wisely!"

Edwards released his hold on Reser's hair and then did something I was not expecting and swiftly stuck the Kabar knife tip in Reser's right nostril and with a flick of his wrist, he cut the boy's nose from the inside out. Edwards then dropped the knife with a clank as blood erupted from Reser's nose on to the pavement.

WHEN THE SONG VANISHES

Reser was still on his stomach and now was holding his nose to keep the blood from flowing. He was not having much luck in that regard. That did not stop him from screaming, "The son of a bitch cut me!"

Edwards slowly stood up and turned toward me and put his hands behind his back. Holstering my weapon, I moved in quickly and handcuffed him. After reading him his rights, I leaned in closer and I asked, "Why did you have to cut him?"

Edwards still calm, replied, "He called me a prairie nigger and a wagon burner! Now each day he looks in the mirror, he will remember the day a Cheyenne Dog Soldier bested him!"

The emergency personnel on-site quickly moved in to tend to Reser and his gushing, notched nose. Looking to John Combs, I said, "As soon as they get the bleeding stopped, arrest Mr. Reser for disturbing the peace and inciting a riot."

As Nickey and I maneuvered Edwards toward the Sheriff's County Blazer for transport, I saw Edwards look over his shoulder and I followed his gaze. He was looking directly at Laney McKay as she stood at the edge of the stage, and she was looking back at him and straight into the young man's eyes. Both of their faces showed pain and regret.

Leaving Nickey at the concert just in case any other disturbances broke out, I transported Edwards by myself. During the thirty-minute drive from Grand Lake to Hot Sulphur Springs, Rod Edwards did not say one word. I kept looking at him in the rearview mirror, and all he did was look out the window as if he was just riding along with me on an enjoyable outing instead of going to jail. Rod Edwards was a genuine piece of work.
Once in the sally port, Edwards was cooperative as the on-duty jailers took him off my hands and placed him in a cell. The next

forty-five minutes I spent filling out the arrest report and detailing everything that I had seen and everything I had said or heard.
In the process of doing my paperwork, John Combs showed up with Kelly Reser and his newly stitched nose. As I saw the jailers stick Reser in the jail cell next to Edwards, I could not help but notice Edwards was right about one thing. The cut was going to scar badly and every time Reser looked in the mirror, it would remind him of his encounter with a Cheyenne Dog Soldier. By the look on Reser's face each time he glanced at Edwards in the cell next to him, I knew that this would be the last time Reser ever tried to bully Edwards.

My thought was Reser had it coming, and if it was up to me, I would just release both of them with a stern lecture. Of course, that was not up to me, and a judge or jury would decide the fate of both young men.

Another hour passed before Nickey made her way into the sheriff's station as the night was coming to an end. According to Nickey, the fight between Edwards and Reser had ended the Laney McKay concert early with Laney visibly upset over what had occurred. As all the Laney McKay fans were leaving Grand Lake, Nickey had a chance to talk with Laney. Nickey said her conversation with Laney was a little strange because she kept asking what would happen to Rod Edwards and where he would be in jail. Laney never once asked about Kelly Reser, the boy that had his nose cut. After hearing Nickey's account of her conversation with Laney, I remembered the look Rod and Laney had exchanged as I was escorting Edwards to the Grand County Sheriff's blazer after I arrested him. At the time I thought the look had more meaning to both of them and now I was sure of it. It made me wonder how well Rod Edwards knew Laney McKay.

CHAPTER 8

Waking up five minutes before the alarm went off, I was in a cold sweat. Another dream of my grandfather and the words, *"Dane, the enemy is not the white warrior"* were still fresh in my memory. Turning off the alarm, I lay there for another fifteen minutes and pushed the dream to the back of my mind. I then focused on the day ahead.

Rolling over to face Nickey's back as she was facing away from me as she was still asleep, I rolled the blanket down off her hip so I could see all her nakedness. Inching in closer, I could smell her essence, and I was reminded once again how much I loved this woman. The last year she had been through so much turmoil, and she had triumphed when most would have crumbled. Taking my forefinger, I slowly traced the outline of her body from the top of her shoulder, down her arm, and then gently over the curvature of her hip. This amorous gesture woke her up, which was my intention. Rolling over on her back, she looked at me with sleepy eyes, and her hand instinctively went to hide the scar on her face. Reaching, I stopped her hand and whispered, "I love you the way you are, and any man would treasure to have you for himself."

Nickey smiled and moved her hand away from her face and lingered it down my body, making my blood rise as she whispered back, "You are just saying that cowboy, because you want some loving. Do we have time?"

"Yes, my love, we have time."

*

Nickey and I drove our separate Grand County Sheriff Blazers to the office in Hot Sulphur Springs. During the morning roll call and brief, which was mostly about the incident at the Laney McKay concert, it surprised me that a lawyer from Denver had already sprung Rod Edwards from jail. To do that, you would have had to wake up a high-powered lawyer in the middle of the night in Denver two and a half hours away and then wake up a Grand County judge in the middle of the night to get the proper documentation to make that happen. It was unheard of. Shaking my head, I could not help but wonder how the hell a mountain Indian without a steady job had the clout and money to accomplish that? Had Laney arranged for Rod to be released?

After Sheriff Tom Walker finished the total day briefing, he asked if anyone had questions, and Nickey was the first one to respond. "Sheriff, it is obvious that Rod Edwards would not have been able to secure his release in the middle of the night. Someone with some money and power must be helping him. I was wondering if you might know who that would be? Is there something else that we are not privy to in this case?"

"Believe me, Nickey, I was as surprised as anyone. All I know is that this sweet-smelling lawyer in a fancy suit showed up here at the same time as I did at 4:30 a.m. with the proper signed documentation from Judge Rick Sullivan to release Mr. Edwards. Mr. Edwards will have his day in court on October 15th. It is not for me to question why I should release him when presented with a judge's order."

WHEN THE SONG VANISHES

My first assignment for the day was eighteen miles to the west in the town of Kremmling. It would seem someone stole a kid's blue and yellow Schwinn sting-ray bike with a banana seat and a high sissy bar. The ten-year-old boy named Rusty Himes was devastated, and he just knew it was that "Rawlings kid" in Granby who had done the dirty deed. I felt for the boy, and I would follow up my investigation with the "Rawlings kid" in Granby.

Taking a call like this was almost refreshing after the recent bank robbery and policing the Laney McKay concert. Maybe I was wrong about my grandfather's dreams and life was returning to normal in Grand County.

After filling out the report, I gave a copy to the parents of the young boy whose bike had been stolen and promised I would follow it up with the Rawlings family in Granby to see if the "kid" somehow ended up with a nice Schwinn bike.

Pulling the Blazer back onto Highway 40 heading east, I plugged in my cassette of Don Williams' "Visions" and my favorite song of his played – "Some Broken Hearts Never Mend."

Rendezvous in the night
A willin' woman to hold me tight
But in the middle of loves embrace
I see your face

Just as I shifted into fourth gear, the police band radio crackled, and Yvonne the dispatcher's voice said, "Undersheriff Lee, and Deputy Lee, Sheriff Walker wants you to head to the Grand Lake Lodge in Grand Lake Village."

I turned off the radio and cassette player and reached for the radio mic. "I am following up a possible stolen bike and heading to Granby. Can I finish that call first?"

Yvonne immediately responded, "Negative Dane, he needs you both to respond immediately. Sheriff Walker will brief you as soon as you get to the Lodge."

Nickey chimed in, "Yvonne, could you give us a few more details on this call at the Grand Lake Lodge?"

Once again Yvonne responded quickly, "Negative, you will be briefed once you get there."

Big mystery and must be important if Sheriff Walker responded to the call first. Looking at my wristwatch and knowing it was a forty-five minute drive for me, I estimated I would get to Grand Lake at around 10:30 a.m.

As I pulled into the parking lot of the historic lodge, it seemed I was the last one to join this gathering of the finest law enforcement officers in Grand County. Nickey's county Blazer was parked next to Sheriff Walker's. The Grand County crime scene van was already on site, and some techs were already taking photographs as some others set up a perimeter around the east side of the lodge. Parking next to Nickey's Blazer, I moved to the room with all the police activity. Sticking my head through the open doorway, I could see the Sheriff and Nickey standing off to the side as the techs moved about cautiously taking photos and gathering evidence. It was obvious that there had been a recent violent struggle within the room as the tables and chairs were overturned and someone had broken a mirror over the bathroom sink. There was no blood visible from my vantage point. Nickey saw me and then got the sheriff's attention, and he turned my way. Sheriff Walker said something to Nickey I could not hear, and she moved in my direction. She pointed out the door, and I moved so she could pass me and then I followed her asking, "What is the big mystery?"
Nickey said, "Right after we left the office, the sheriff's department got a call from Laney's manager about 9:00 am that she was missing and that her room was in disarray."

"I thought Laney was heading to the Stapleton airport in Denver after the concert."

"Laney's manager said she changed her mind and wanted to stick around a few days here in Grand County to see someone, and she did not want anyone to know that she was still here."

I could not help but remember that look that Rod Edwards had exchanged with Laney while I was arresting him. What was the connection between the two other than they both were from Grand County? My gut instinct was telling me that the Cheyenne Dog Soldier was smack dab in the middle of Laney's disappearance. How he was involved, I did not have a clue at this point. Was this a kidnapping and ransom demand? Had Laney been murdered for revenge or lust? One thing for sure was once the papers got a hold of the fact that the number one country singer in America had vanished, this town once again would be under siege from the national media. The look of deep thought was on Nickey's face and showed she was just as worried as I was about our friend. "Nickey, do we know yet who she was wanting to see? Was there any blood found in her room?"

"Negative on both. I have asked myself one question since early this morning. Who would have money and clout in Grand County to get Rod Edwards released from jail so quickly?"

By the all-knowing look on Nickey's face, she already thought she knew, and she wanted to see if I came up with the same answer. Hearing Nickey ask the question out loud, it seemed to come clear in my mind. "The only person with that kind of money and clout right now would be Laney McKay."

Nickey nodded her head and then replied, "Exactly!"
Nickey and I nodded our heads in agreement when Sheriff Walker came rushing out of the room and quickly made his way toward us. "I just questioned the cleaning lady who is a local. She said she had seen Rod Edwards in the parking lot this morning."

CHAPTER 9

Sheriff Walker seemed perplexed with this fresh development since Rod Edwards was just released this morning at 4:30 a.m. I remembered the call from Laney's manager came in at 9:00 a.m. meaning if Rod Edwards was involved in Laney's disappearance, it happened early this morning. Sheriff Walker finally decided, "Dane, are you familiar with Rod Edwards' living arrangements?"

"He lives with his mother Isabella in a cabin in the Never Summer Mountains, west of Rocky Mountain National Park. I used to hunt elk in that area, and I know exactly where the cabin is. Rod's dad died about ten years ago, and Rod and his mother have been living up there by themselves ever since."

Sheriff Walker pointed toward my county Blazer. "To be honest we are not sure a crime has been committed here, but the circumstances of Laney being as famous as she is, we are going to treat it as if there has been a crime. I need you and Nickey to hightail out to the Edwards' place and have a look see. If Edwards is there with Laney, bring them both back! If Edwards is there without Laney, arrest him and bring him in! If neither of them is there, talk to Isabella and see what she knows. I will get on the radio and get a warrant ready for Edwards' arrest just in case we need it! My hope is we can settle this matter before the press gets involved."

The easiest access to the Edwards' cabin was from Rocky Mountain National Park, taking Highway 34 until we reached the Kawuneeche Valley entrance. From there, we followed Trail Ridge Road to the Bowen/Baker Trailhead, which was the easiest route to the Never Summer Mountains.

The Never Summer Mountains supply water to the Colorado River, the North Platte River, and the Cache la Poudre River. It was a remote wilderness area with ranges from forested ridges to steep tundra. Altitudes ranged from 8,900 to 12,580 feet in elevation. The Never Summer Mountains are a sight to behold. And with peak names such as Cirrus, Stratus, Cumulus, and Nimbus, there's no denying that the peaks are tucked amidst the clouds. The Never Summer wilderness area got its name from the massive amounts of snow and rain the area regularly experiences, but this weather provides for some diverse wilderness. Some of the most fascinating wilderness in this area was to the north where ponds and bogs create rare habitats for creatures including wood frogs, bog bean, pygmy shrews, and even wolves. The area's moisture that helps create these habitats also supports exceptionally large and old spruce and fir trees, the largest of which can get up to four feet in diameter, and the oldest of which has been estimated at 600 years old.

Looking above at the timberline, I estimated we were standing at about 9500 feet in elevation. The day had cooled considerably with dark and menacing clouds moving in, and the temperature was now just above freezing and cold enough that we could see our breath.

It was midafternoon when we reached the trailhead just east of the Edwards' cabin. I stopped and Nickey and I got out with our field binoculars and walked over to the edge of the evergreens and found a clear line of sight toward the Edwards' homestead. There were three buildings and several corrals that were visible and were as I remembered it. The lodge pole cabin was the main house; there was a large lodge pole barn and the remaining building looked to be a newer stick built three car garage. There was smoke rising from the stone chimney above the cabin, indicating someone was home. There was a 1972 Chevy blue and white two-tone pickup sitting in front of the main house, but no other vehicles out in the open. Still watching for movement down below, Nickey asked, "How do you want to play this?"

"The only way we can is to just drive to the main house and have a look see as the sheriff asked."

Nickey lowered her field glasses and looked at me. "How well do you know Isabella Edwards?"

"Isabella has lived in the Never Summer Mountains her entire life. Both she and Rod's dad were/are full blood Cheyenne Indians. This area is their tribal ancestral home that dates back before the Spanish or white men walked these mountains of old. Her husband Jim died years ago in a mountain lion attack. Some say Jim was a Cheyenne Dog Soldier in a long line of Dog Soldiers, and that training and creed had been passed down to his son Rod. After seeing Rod in action the other night, I would say that he has the mentality and the ability to belong to the order of the fiercest warriors of the Cheyenne Nation. To answer your question, Isabella Edwards is a good and resourceful woman. She is tougher than nails and intelligent, but isolated from the trappings of any town or city. Don't feel sorry for her though, for it is the life she wants - she is one with nature here. Let's head on in and I will introduce you to her."

Pulling slowly on to the Edwards' property, Nickey and I tried to scrutinize everything to see if anything might seem out of kilter. A small Indian woman, with long dark hair with a wonderful mixture of grey woven into two long braids that reached down to her waist, appeared on the front porch. In her hands she held a lever action Henry rifle, and there was no doubt in my mind she knew how to use it. It wasn't until Nickey and I stepped out of the Blazer that a broad smile crossed her face and she leaned the rifle up against a support post. "What a pleasant surprise. Always nice when a handsome man such as Dane Lee comes to visit an old woman. What brings you into the Never Summer Mountains, Dane?"

A smile crossed my face because I always liked and adored Isabella. "You are looking fit as a fiddle Isabella and that warms my heart. Actually, as you probably have guessed, this is not a social call, but we are here on sheriff business. We need to talk to Rod if he is home."

The smile evaporated from Isabella's face as she spoke, "Haven't seen Rod in several days. His girl is back in town, and he went to courting. He was supposed to bring her out here last night late, but I have not seen hide nor hair of them yet, nor has he called."

So, Rod had a girlfriend, or at least that is what he told his mother. "Do you know his girlfriend's name?"

Laughing, Isabella said, "Of course I do you dimwit; they have been seeing each other since way back in high school. Her family lives in Granby, and her name is Laney McKay."

Nickey quickly asked, "You mean Laney McKay, the singer?" Isabella still smiling asked, "Sorry, not sure we have met. What is your name?"

I almost laughed as Nickey stumbled to answer because the question took her off guard. "My apologies, Mrs. Edwards. My name is Nickey Lynn Lee."

Isabella's eyebrows lifted on hearing the name and then waved her finger back and forth from me to Nickey. "Lee? Does that mean you are married to each other?"

Letting Nickey handle this as she answered, "Yes, Dane and I have been married almost a year now."

Isabella moved closer to Nickey as she looked into my wife's eyes and reached up and gently touched the scar on her face. To my disbelief, Nickey let her without removing her hand. Isabella closed her eyes as she continued touching the scar on Nickey's face for a full minute. Finally, Isabella removed her hand and opened her eyes and a tear rolled down her face. To my surprise, Nickey's face was wet with a tear of her own. Whatever just happened was magical. That moment in time, Nickey and the older Cheyenne Indian woman made a connection like no other. It brought a tear to my eye as well. Isabella still locked onto Nickey's eyes, said, "You are so special and beautiful Nickey. I felt your pain and misery that you experienced. You are strong to come back from the evil that had tried to take your soul and life. You have come a long way in such a short time. I also feel your happiness with Dane, for he is special as well. The both of you together can stand the winds of time. I am so happy you have found the other!" Isabella stepped forward and hugged Nickey, and Nickey returned the hug like they were kin and had known each other their entire lives. It really was quite beautiful. After another full minute, Isabella stepped back holding Nickey's hands and said, "To answer your question, yes, Laney has a voice like an angel. She used to come here and bring her guitar, and she would sing for me all the time. She really is something special, and I love her dearly. I would tell her all the time that her musical talent would take her places if she applied herself. Since she took that job back east in Tennessee, I only get to see her once or twice a year now. I worry about her and Rod's relationship since she took that job. Although, my belief is if their pairing is supposed to be, then the spirits will make it so."

It was obvious to both Nickey and me that Isabella, being as isolated that she was here in the Never Summer Mountains, did not know that the "job in Tennessee" meant that Laney McKay was the most famous country singer in the United States and probably in the world. I for one would not tell her since it really was not my place. If Laney never told her, then it meant to me that this one of the last places in the world that Laney could go and just be that young girl from Middle Park High school and just be Laney

McKay without the lights and the fans. This was her sanctuary, and I would not intrude on that.

The problem I was facing now with this wonderful woman of the mountains was that her son may have caused harm to Laney. Without all the facts, it was leaning in that direction. Laney and Rod were missing, and there had been a violent struggle in Laney's room at the Grand Lake Lodge. You had two sweethearts from high school with Laney becoming not only famous, but very wealthy. Laney had become the talk of Nashville and Hollywood and was now a citizen of the world. Rod probably would not leave these mountains and he barely functioned in towns like Granby or Grand Lake. I could not even fathom how much stress Laney's success had to be on the two young lovers' relationship. One had to wonder after Rod had gotten released from jail, did he quarrel with Laney and in a fit of rage do something that can't be undone? I was worried before, but now the more I thought about it, Laney could possibly be dead. If Laney McKay was still alive, she was in serious trouble, and we needed to locate her quickly.

It was obvious from Isabella's reaction to Nickey's and my arrival that she knew nothing about where Rod or Laney might be. Knowing time was of the essence, I said to Isabella, "Isabella if Rod or Laney show up here, tell them to contact the sheriff's department immediately. Someone reported Laney as missing, and we were just following up on that report. It might be nothing at all, but we have to do our jobs."

Isabella's face showed concern, "Dane should I be worried?"

My voice betrayed me by sounding concerned myself, "We are not sure yet Isabella, but that may ring true."

CHAPTER 10

Once Nickey and I were seated in the Blazer, I looked to the horizon and knew there were only about three hours of sunlight left and we still did not have a good lead on the disappearance of Laney McKay. Looking at Nickey, I could see the frustration on her face as well. Pushing the gas pedal a little too heavy, I spun the tires and sprayed some gravel as I backed up. Now engaging the clutch and shifting into second, I sprayed some more gravel as we pulled out of the driveway of the Edwards' homestead.

About a mile away from our meeting with Isabella Edwards, I could see Nickey touching the scar on her face. I said, "Isabella is an amazing woman. Seeing you and her together was almost mystical in some ways."

Nickey turned toward me, and another tear rolled down her face. It was as if she entered my soul and walked softly among all my haunts and dreams. I have experienced nothing like that before. It did not scare me at all; it actually gave me a sense of relief that I have not felt since the attack. Now knowing Rod's mom in such a manner, I struggled to believe that her son would ever be capable of hurting Laney, but then I remembered Rod cutting the nose of that other guy, marking him for life. Rod Edwards is hard to figure out.

"Just remember, Nickey that first and foremost Rod Edwards is a Cheyenne Dog Soldier with training from the United States Special

WHEN THE SONG VANISHES

Forces. He is a warrior and very dangerous, regardless of how his mother is."

Another mile down the road, the police radio crackled twice with some very loud static and then returned to silence. I knew someone had just broadcasted, but in these mountains the reception was often piss poor. Another mile and the radio static returned, but this time with the voice of Yvonne the dispatcher floating on the static air wave, "Undersheriff Lee, if you get this message the sheriff needs a word with you. It is urgent!"

I pulled off to the side of the road and stopped since I had reception. "Dispatch, this is Dane, put the sheriff on. I have reception now."

The radio crackled and hissed, and then Sheriff Walker's voice came on, "Be advised, we had a call that the female you are inquiring about was seen this morning north of the North Supply Trailhead. Also, sending Deputy Combs and Mason with provisions and details."

Depressing the mic's button, "Understood, and understood!" Nickey looked at me with some confusion. "What the hell was that?"

Smiling, I said, "Half of Grand County citizens own police scanners, and since the media has not been informed of Laney's disappearance yet, he was being cautious in what he was trying to tell us. What I gathered from what he said is that Laney was spotted north of the North Supply Trailhead. John Combs and Deputy Mason are going to meet us there with more detail and emergency backpacks since it is late in the day, and we might be spending the night in the woods."

Nickey lifting her eyebrows said, "A night in the woods with my cowboy; I sort of like that idea."

The good news was if the report was correct, then Laney was more than likely still alive. What we did not know is if Laney was alone or with someone. There was a good possibility that no crime had been committed, and all this worrying and searching was for naught. I hoped that was the case, but my gut instinct was telling me differently. We would know more when we hooked up with the other deputies.

If we had the ability to fly over the top of the deep, dark timber such as a crow, we could have been to the North Supply Trailhead in twenty minutes. Since we did not have that capability, it took us forty-five minutes to reach the remote trailhead. The trailhead was empty with no vehicles since we had reached it before John Combs and the other deputy being dispatched by the department.
With only about two hours of sunlight left, the temperature was dropping as Nickey and I sat in the Blazer with the heater running listening to the cassette player when one of our favorite renditions of a great song "Suspicious Minds" - this one by Waylon Jennings & Jessi Colter - started playing The song got me thinking of Laney McKay and her boyfriend Rod Edwards.

We're caught in a trap, I can't walk out
Because I love you too much, baby
Why can't you see what you're doing to me?
Oh, when you don't believe a word I'm saying?

Thinking of that verse, I could not help but wonder if Laney was caught in a trap she could not get out of. Just as the final lyrics faded, deputies John Combs and Barry Mason pulled up in John's Grand County Blazer.

Barry Mason was a young redhead with freckles and a recent graduate of the police academy. He was not the biggest fellow at about 5'10" and if he weighed 160 pounds, it was because he had rocks in his pockets. Working for Grand County was his first law enforcement job, and he had only been with the department for about two months. He was a good and eager kid and if we started off into the woods in a rescue/search operation, I would have to keep my eye on him since to the best of my knowledge he was a city boy with no wood craft ability.

We all got out of our Blazers, and John Combs made a beeline for Nickey and me. He seemed enthusiastic as he caught us up to date with what Sheriff Walker could not say on the radio. "Sheriff Walker got a call from a couple of locals scouting the area for elk. They said they were looking down from the mountain with their field glasses onto North Supply Creek searching for elk, and they saw a woman running with a dark-haired man alongside the creek heading east. They did not get a good look at the man, but they swore the woman was none other than Laney McKay. In my pocket I have a warrant for the arrest of Rod Edwards for the possible kidnap of Laney McKay. Sheriff wanted the best tracker in Colorado in the woods at the crack of dawn scouting along North Supply Creek hoping to cut their sign to track them."
It was highly possible I could find their trail, but if it was Edwards and he had kidnapped Laney, he would have the skill and the training to hide his trail and move through the forest as a ghost. This hunt or search and rescue was to be a throwback to the old ways of Edwards' ancestors the Cheyenne, and my ancestors the Utes, when they were at war with each other's tribes. Looking north toward where I knew North Supply Creek was, I said, "Did you bring the emergency packs?"

John replied quickly, "Yes, we grabbed four, one for each of us; they are in the back of my Blazer. We also have two five-gallon water jugs that are full."

Grand County Sheriff Department emergency packs were backpacks that were not gender specific but held the essentials for one person to survive in relative comfort for five days in the wilderness. Most of the time the deputies used them when we had to deploy into the field looking for those tourists that have gotten lost in the remote mountains in Grand County. Each pack contained a poly-filled sleeping bag; two-man pup tent; small propane camp stove; three bottles of propane; compass; map of

Grand County; canteen; fold up mess kit with eating utensils; first aid kit; signaling mirror; whistle; silver-sided emergency blanket; twelve feet of rope; pocket knife; one set of clothing with underwear and three pairs of socks; waterproof matches; fire starter kit, and fifteen Mountain House freeze-dried meals. Earlier, while sitting in the Blazer listening to Waylon and Jessi, I had spotted a small clearing about thirty yards north of our position and I now pointed toward it. "Since there is only a little more than an hour of daylight left, I want to set up camp in that clearing. While you are all getting set up, I am going to use what light there is left and scout on up to North Supply Creek and try to cut any sign of anyone recently using the trail there."

Grabbing my Ruger Mini-14 rifle from its scabbard just behind my seat in the Blazer, I then loaded it with the required .223 caliber ammo. I also grabbed an extra .223 ammo bandolier and slid that over my shoulder. Having done that, I quick palmed my 357 Ruger Blackhawk and made sure it was fully loaded in the bean wheel. Holstering the Blackhawk, I then grabbed a set of field glasses and with a quick nod toward Nickey, I moved silently into the dark timber north of our campsite and moved north towards North Supply Creek.

Once in the woods, I felt at home. It was Indian blood in me that the wilderness spoke to, and as I cautiously moved north, my senses became in tune with all that surrounded me. I could feel the temperature change downward a degree at a time, and my eyes became accustomed to the low light of the day and my hearing became more acute. Not far in the distance ahead of me, I could hear the trickle of the water as it flowed down through the creek. Twenty yards from the creek, there was a fairly large clearing about a quarter of a mile across. Still staying in the tree line and not exposing myself, I used my field glasses to follow and explore the meadow and the surrounding tree line, looking for movement. Slowly searching the ever-changing shadows because of the low light, I saw nothing of interest until I was half-way through my search grid, and I saw a flash of red. Moving the glasses back to the spot, I had seen the red and then…nothing. I knew I saw it, so I kept the glasses trained on that spot and a small gust of wind exposed the red again…bright red.

Concentrating harder on the spot, I finally realized what I was looking at was a camouflaged net draped over a fairly large object at the edge of the clearing. The wind had moved the netting just enough for several seconds at a time to expose the red beneath it. Smiling to myself, I thought I knew what was hidden beneath the netting. There were only about forty minutes of daylight left as I moved swiftly across the clearing. As I got closer, it became more obvious that I was correct in my assumption of what was below the netting. With one quick pull, I yanked the netting over to one side and exposed the bright red helicopter beneath it. It would seem in my search for Laney, I had inadvertently come across the elusive two-seater Enstrom F-28C helicopter that had been used by the radical Insurgence members in their get-away from the bank robbery in Grand Lake.

As I looked up into the encroaching night sky, it was obvious there was no way anyone searching for the Insurgence or this helicopter could have seen it during a fly over. It was just good luck that I was looking at the right spot at the exact time that the wind had moved the netting just a hair to expose the bright red paint. Leaving the netting pulled back and part of the helicopter exposed, I stepped out into the clearing and watched the dying sun of the day as it dropped below the western horizon in all its blue and orange glory as I thought about Laney McKay. It was too dark to begin the search, and all I could hope for was that Laney was some place safe, warm, and secure.

CHAPTER 11

An hour after finding the Insurgence's helicopter, I walked into the campsite where Nickey, John, and Barry had set up in my absence. There were three pup tents set up since Nickey and I would share; in addition, they had a good warming fire roaring. Nickey asked me what I wanted for dinner - freeze-dried spaghetti and meatballs or freeze-dried pot roast. I pointed to the pot roast as she dumped the contents into a mess kit pan and then added boiling water that had heated on the fire. Finding a spot on the log that Nickey was sitting on, I sat down right next to her as she handed me my supper and a canteen of water.

Mountain House freeze-dried foods had been developed for our troops in Vietnam to replace the old-style C-rations that were common in World War II and the Korean War. After Vietnam, Mountain House sold their surplus to sporting goods stores, and they quickly became the staple of outdoorsmen. Taking a bite of the pot roast, I realized how hungry I was and quickly downed the whole bowl full along with a full canteen of water. Nickey and the others waited until I was finished before John asked, "Did you have any luck cutting their trail?"

WHEN THE SONG VANISHES

"No, I didn't, but I found something very interesting in a clearing right next to North Supply Creek!"

Nickey raised her eyebrows and then asked, "Well, spit it out. What exactly did you find?"

Laughing, I said, "I found the helicopter that the Insurgence used during the Grand Mountain Bank robbery."

There was total silence for almost a full minute as everyone stared at me in disbelief followed by Nickey shoving me hard, saying, "Get out of here! You did not!"

Nickey's shove sent me over the log, and I fell on my back. Everyone started laughing, including myself; I righted myself and climbed back onto the log. "I am not joking; I found the helicopter. It was hidden under a camouflaged netting. Those Kansas boys must have stashed their getaway vehicles here at the trailhead and then hightailed it out of here after stashing the helicopter."

John said it first before Nickey could, "You are serious! You found the helicopter?"

"Serious as a heart attack!"

Nickey laughed out loud, "Imagine that - all of them FBI boys roaming the countryside and doing those flyovers and with all their high-tech gear and dogs, they could not find a trace of the Insurgence. Then along comes my slow talking and rambling husband who spends an hour in the woods and "bang" he finds the helicopter."

"Slow talking and rambling?"

Nickey leaned over and kissed me on the cheek. "Yes, honey, you got that mountain drawl and that John Wayne sway of your hips when you walk."

That got everyone laughing again. Everyone was in a good mood since there was a good reason to believe Laney McKay was alive and also that someone had seen her this morning. Nickey, John, and Barry seemed to enjoy the company of each other, and this felt like an overnight camping trip with friends instead of a search and rescue. I was not so sure. As the others started to shoot the shit and talk as they sat around the campfire, I started thinking ahead on what needed to be done come first light.

I was thinking to myself and only half listening to the others' conversation. We still had to treat this as a crime in progress with Rod Edwards as a kidnapper. Just as I ran that scenario through my mind, something John Combs was telling Barry Mason caught my attention. All ears now, I turned to John and asked, "What did you just say?"

I caught John off guard with my question and he blinked his eyes several times and then asked, "What?"

"What did you just say?"

In a hesitant voice John spoke, "I was telling Barry, the city boy here, about Cheyenne Dog Soldiers is all."

"I gathered that. How did you describe them again?"

John was still confused on where this conversation was going. "I was telling him the brief history that I know, and I said that folks down through the years called them Cheyenne Dog Soldiers, Dog Soldiers, and White Warriors."

Hearing John's words once again, my grandfather's voice and the dream came flooding back into my memory, *"Dane, the enemy is not the white warrior!"*

WHEN THE SONG VANISHES

I had forgotten that the Dog Soldiers were sometimes called White Warriors because they sometimes painted their entire bodies white before they went into battle to seem ghostlike and to create fear in the face of their enemies. How could I forget that? That is what my grandfather was trying to tell me. Rod Edwards was not the enemy here. If Rod Edwards was not the enemy, then who was? This new and old information filtered through my mind as I stood up with a realization. How could I be so stupid! Pointing at the fire, I said, "Put the fire out now!"

Nickey had stood up when I did, and she grabbed my arm gently and asked, "Dane, what is the issue? Are you okay?"

Turning to look at her, I saw her confusion. "John described a dog soldier as a white warrior! I have been so stupid! Don't you get it? In my grandfather's dream, he told me the white warrior was not the enemy! Rod Edwards is not the enemy here. I don't know what he is, but he is not the enemy! He did not kidnap Laney!"

Nickey shook her head as if she was trying to clear cobwebs. "If Edwards is not the problem, then who is?"

"The helicopter! The damn red helicopter! I believe the Insurgence bandits are still here! My guess those Kansas boys never left and that they have been hiding out here, somewhere close. We need to put out the fire and call in the Calvary!"

Nickey's face lit up as what I just said sank in, and she realized the danger we might all be in. She and I had fought only one of the Insurgence members and came out on the losing side. Now there might be six of those bastards out in the woods not far off.

Nickey grabbed one of the collapsible camp shovels and started shoveling dirt onto the fire to extinguish it. John and Barry had no idea what the hell was going on but saw our urgency and quickly joined in to help Nickey douse the fire.

Grabbing my police radio off my belt, I depressed the side transmit button. "Dispatch, this is Undersheriff Lee. Do you copy?"

Nothing but static. I tried once more, "Dispatch, this is Undersheriff Lee. Do you copy?" Still nothing but static. Just as I feared, we were in a transmission dead spot.

Placing my radio back on my belt, I pondered on the next course of action when I saw movement in the dark timber before me. Quickly palming my Ruger pistol, I pointed in the area where I saw the movement and to my absolute surprise Laney McKay and Rod Edwards emerged out of the dark timber and deep shadows. Both looked rough as hell. Laney's hair was ratted with pine needles and small twigs. Both were caked in wet and dried mud. Edwards was also holding a Henry lever action carbine rifle in his hands.

Nickey and the others had extinguished the campfire, and there was only the light of the moon to see by. As my eyes adjusted to the near darkness, I moved my pistol to cover Edwards and said, "Drop the rifle Edwards, you are under arrest!"

Nickey, John, and Barry now joined me, and all three also palmed their service weapons and had them pointed at Rod Edwards. Even in the low light, I could see anger cross the face of Rod, and I knew there was no way he was going to drop his rifle. As the tension of the moment built, Laney slowly moved in front of Edwards with her hand up to her chest with the palms out. "Whoa everyone, take a breather. Dane, please lower your pistol. Rod has done nothing wrong. Matter of fact he saved me from those other men!"

"Okay Laney, before we lower our weapons, give me the short version of what the hell is going on!"
Laney moved closer so I could see her better. Rod was still on edge and kept looking behind him into the trees in the direction Laney and he had come from but remained where he was, holding the carbine. His Henry rifle was now pointed toward the ground, and his focus was not really on us standing before him but on the

woods that surrounded us. Edwards knew, and my gut instinct was telling me that the danger was not with each other but was just beyond the tree line in the shadows of the night. Laney cleared her voice, "Rod has been my boyfriend since high school. After Rod had been arrested and I returned to my hotel room after the concert, I called my attorney in Denver so he could make arraignments for Rod to make bail and be released. I gave my attorney instructions to tell Rod to meet me at the Grand Lake Lodge once he got out. Knowing that would take a while, I went to bed. When I woke up this morning, there were two men in my room. I was scared to death as one man held a gun to my head as the other one calmly told me they were there to kidnap me. He told me they would not harm me and that the only reason I was being kidnapped was to be held for ransom and that I would not be violated and would be released unharmed once they had their money. They were going to contact my record label and demand one million dollars for my safe return!"

I was close enough to see Laney's eyes and could see she was telling the truth. Nodding my head toward the others, I holstered my weapon as did they. "I am a little confused - all we got from your manager was that you were missing; we were never told of a ransom demand."

"Probably because Rod rescued me before they could get me to wherever they were going to hold me. They never had a chance to ask for a ransom."

Rod stepped forward and in a clear, but urgent voice, "Dane, we need to move now! These fellows are looking for Laney and they have training! They are not Indian, but they move through the woods as you and I do. Military training, probably Special Forces. I have been able to elude them a couple of times today, but they have always found our trail again. I am assuming your vehicles are at the trailhead. We need to get them and get the hell out of here now!"

Looking at Barry, John, and Nickey, I said in a quiet voice, "Pack up quietly, we are leaving now."

Laney joined the others and quickly went about packing up camp. I turned back to Rod and looked him straight in the eye. "Fill me in Edwards on how you knew Laney had been kidnapped."

With a flash of anger, Rod's eyes narrowed. "You don't trust me, Dane; I get it, but no big mystery here. After getting released, I headed to the Grand Lake Lodge as Laney had asked. Sometimes I let my anger get the best of me, and I knew I had disappointed Laney in what happened. Once at the lodge, I saw Laney and two men heading out the door of Laney's room and getting into a 1974 gold Buick Apollo. I had no idea she was being kidnapped; I thought the men might be her managers or possibly hired security and bodyguards. Not being alarmed, I followed them, hoping to catch Laney by herself to apologize for what happened at the concert. Once they were in Rocky Mountain National Park, I kept my distance as they parked the car in a remote area campground. I was about one mile away and watched through my field binoculars. Both men got out of the car, and one man roughly pulled Laney out; it was then I saw they had her hands tied. Grabbing my Henry rifle from my pickup, I moved into the timber to stay off the road and made my way in their direction, hoping I could ghost up on them before they drove off again. One man had ventured off into the woods and during the time I was moving toward them, he never returned. The lone man now left guarding Laney stepped behind a tree to take a piss, and that is when I waylaid him with the butt of my rifle. I would have shot him but feared the gunfire would attract the first man's attention. Thinking back on it, I should have cut his throat, but didn't. I grabbed Laney and took to the timber and tried making our way back to my truck. By the time we were halfway there, two men found the one I had knocked out, and three others drove the road and found my truck. All six men including the one I rifle butted took to the timber from behind us, looking for tracks we may have left or any sign of our movements. It was then I realized these guys had skills, woodcraft skills. Since my truck was no longer an option, we turned south and have been on the run and eluding them all day until we smelled your campfire."

Just as Rod was finishing up his side of the story, Nickey, Laney, Barry and John joined us, and we started for the trailhead when a deep voice came out of the darkness to the north, "You folks, hold it right there!"

Barry had already pulled his service pistol as we started toward the trailhead and our Grand County Blazers. It was a fatal mistake; Barry Mason and the rookie deputy sheriff panicked and with no target he fired in the voice's direction. One shot rang out from the woods followed by the sound as if someone had dropped a watermelon. Barry Mason dropped heavily to the ground! Even in the moon light, I could tell someone had shot him in the head from close range. Barry Mason was dead.

CHAPTER 12

The voice sounded again, "Stand down! We are coming in and will kill anyone that goes for their weapon."

There could be as many as six armed and very dangerous men surrounding us. It would seem they had us at the disadvantage, and for now there was nothing to do but comply with their demands until an opportunity presented itself. Looking at the slumped body of Barry Mason angered me to no end. Speaking loudly enough for everyone to hear, "Nobody go for their weapons, I mean nobody!"

After I turned my focus toward the direction that voice had come from, one man stepped into the small clearing where we now found ourselves. The moon had risen high in the night sky, and the clouds were absent so there was now plenty of light to see by; the man who stood before us was none other than Clarence O'Brien the ex-marine medic; he looked just like his photo. The briefing from the FBI had all the Insurgence members' photos, and I had studied them all closely. O'Brien, dressed in Levis and a flannel shirt with a sheepskin coat, held in his hand an Israeli Uzi submachine gun pointed in our direction. The Uzi had a shoulder sling attached to it so he could easily let it ride when using the 45 caliber MIP11A1 Colt automatic pistol in a holster on his right hip. From the direction the slug that killed Barry came from, it had to be Clarence O'Brien who had killed the deputy, probably with his

WHEN THE SONG VANISHES

Colt 45. Given the chance, I would make O'Brien pay for that. Another man who dressed similarly as O'Brien had also emerged from the timber behind us. Glancing back, I could see the man behind us, and I recognized him from his photo even though he had recently taken the butt end of Rod Edwards' Henry rifle dead center of his face. It was Bob Jonasen, the ex-ranger that served with the Long Range Reconnaissance Patrol.

Both Insurgence radicals were armed with an Uzi and a 45 caliber Colt automatic pistol. O'Brien looked none too happy as he spoke, "This entire day has been a disaster. Now I need you all very slowly, and I mean slowly, lay your weapons in the dirt."

I turned and looked at Nickey, Rod, John, and Laney and not one of them showed fear. It pissed all of them off that we were being made to comply. Seeing no choice but to comply, I nodded to all of them and reluctantly they laid their pistols and rifles at their feet. I noticed Edwards had not given up his Kabar combat knife and neither did I. My Kabar was in its sheath, attached to my belt on my right side and hidden by my coat.

Reaching down inside his sheepskin coat, O'Brien produced a walkie-talkie. Obviously the other four members were not with these two members of the Insurgence, but probably not far behind. Since the other member of the radicals were in the same valley as we were, O'Brien would not experience the same problems of establishing contact as I had trying to reach our office in Hot Sulphur Springs twenty-seven miles away. Depressing the call button, there was a slight crackle of static, and then O'Brien spoke, "Dan, we have McKay. There are five others with her; four of them are deputies of the Grand County Sheriff's department. There has been one casualty."
Several seconds passed and then the radio hissed and crackled, and Dan responded, "Have you disabled their vehicles and radios? We heard the gunshot. Who was the casualty?"

O'Brien answered, "All vehicles disabled with flat tires; Jonasen slashed every tire. Radio antennas of vehicles disabled as well. One deputy is the casualty."

"Shit! Do not shoot anyone else. I will decide what to do once we get there. We are inbound to your position with an ETA of twenty-five minutes."

Hearing the last radio transmission, I knew that after the rest of the Insurgence members made an appearance, it would be game over. Whatever needed to be done to give us a chance of escape needed to happen now! Looking over my shoulder, I caught Rod Edwards' eye, and he blinked twice, showing he understood it was now or never. Rod then slowly turned toward Bob Jonasen and said, "Never knew taking a rifle butt to the face could improve one's looks, but here we are."

Jonasen's eyes narrowed as he responded, "Your ass is mine, Indian when the others get here!"

Rolling his eyes, Rod almost laughed, "Others? Figured as much that you could not handle me by yourself, old man!"

That was enough to cause the radical to make a mistake as he dropped the Uzi and let it hang by the shoulder strap. Jonasen quickly produced a fighting knife. "You got lucky the first time, boy! Now I am going to teach you a lesson!"

Just as Jonasen made his first step forward, Edwards produced his own fighting knife. What Jonasen did not know was he was now facing a skilled warrior of the Cheyenne nation - a Dog Soldier! As all eyes focused on Edwards and Jonasen, O'Brien swung his Uzi toward Edwards, which gave me my opening. Pulling my Kabar, I rushed O'Brien and before he could recover and point the Uzi in my direction, I slammed into him with all my body weight which took him off his feet so hard that the back of his head hit the ground before his shoulders. O'Brien had lost his grip on the Uzi, but still had enough of his reasoning and wherewithal to pull his own knife for close combat. Since my body was on top of his, he tried a downward thrust to stab me in the back, which nicked my right arm as I rolled to my left. During mid-roll, I thrust my knife upward into the chest of O'Brien. Once the knife penetrated all the way to the hilt, I turned it several times, hoping to nick my assailant's heart. Feeling O'Brien's body go slack, I removed my knife and separated from him. Scooting backward on my butt, I could see that O'Brien's eyes were fading out as his life slowly bled away.

Realizing I was not the only one who had been in a fight to the death, I swiftly looked toward Edwards and Jonasen. Edwards was still on his feet covered in blood, as was Jonasen. Edwards was breathing deeply, trying to catch his breath; Jonasen staggered and then collapsed and would never breathe again.

Thankful there had been no gunshots to alert the remaining four members of the Insurgence, I stood quickly as Nickey, John, and Laney recovered their weapons. Now standing beside Rod, I asked, "Rod, where is the nearest telephone? We need to call in for help!"

With some difficulty, Edwards stood straight up and grimaced when he responded, "At my mom and dad's place; mom had a phone installed right after my dad died. With your vehicles having their tires slashed, the quickest way there is up the Edwards Sluice."

Although I couldn't see it in the darkness, I looked south toward Edwards Sluice. Edwards Sluice, as the crow flies, was more than a mile to the south. Locals and Grand County natives called it the Edwards Sluice because the Edwards homestead was directly at the top. The natural sluice was like a knife cut into the mountain in the shape of a narrow "V" that went from the top of the mountain to the bottom. Edwards Sluice had been created naturally when heavy rain or snowmelt used the pathway to shed the mountain of its water. During both rain and heavy snowmelt, the sluice was just like a raging river. It would be my guess for every six feet horizontally it rose ten feet vertically. The sluice was not a waterfall when full of water or even an equivalent of climbing a mountain when not, but it was damn close to both. Of course, just like any riverbed it was full of granite rocks and boulders, most of them loose from when the water did flow through it. The sluice would be a dangerous climb in the daylight and even worse in the dark. Running this throughout my mind, I turned back to Edwards, and he grimaced again before speaking, "I know what you are thinking, Dane. It is a dangerous climb in the dark, but it is the fastest route to a phone right now. If you are worried about Laney, don't be. She and I have been climbing that sluice ever since we were kids, many times in the dark. Let Laney take point; she knows where the best handholds are."

Feeling time was wasting away and the other radicals of the Insurgence would be here soon, I responded, "I agree, it is the best plan for now. We better get moving."

Picking up Jonasen's Uzi and stripping him of his pistol and spare magazines, I handed them to Edwards. I grabbed O'Brien's weapons and ammo for myself. I then quickly explained to the others what we were going to do. Since Laney actually knew the lay of the land better than everyone other than Rod, I had her go first, then Nickey, and then John. When I suggested to Rod that he go next, he refused and said he needed to be the one that brought up the rear guard. Looking at the dead Insurgence member at his feet, I could hardly argue with that. After reaching down, I took Barry Mason's badge and stuck it in my pocket. Gently, I closed his eyes and whispered, "You got a raw deal Barry, and I will be back for you."

Taking one last look at Rod Edwards, I hustled after John with Rod close behind me.

CHAPTER 13

The night sky was still cloudless with an almost full moon to provide light to see. Having enough light to see was great for us in one way but could be our undoing in another way because the moon also provided light for those that would start to hunt us once they found both of their men dead.

The air was chilled but refreshing when we took deep breaths. Laney surprised me as she moved through the woods. It was obvious that being in a relationship with Edwards, he taught her some woodcraft skills.

We were making good time and were about half-way to the bottom of Edwards Sluice when I looked behind me and saw Rod stumble and almost go down. Something was wrong. Speaking just loudly enough that John could hear me, "We need to stop, John. Pass it on up through Nickey to Laney."

Moving quietly back to Rod, "Are you okay?"
Rod looked me straight in the eye, and I could see that he was in a lot of pain. "Not really, Dane."

The Cheyenne Dog Soldier took a step back and leaned against an evergreen tree and then pulled his coat open. What he showed me was not good news. It would seem that before Rod had killed Jonasen that the radical had stabbed Rod in his stomach. What Rod showed me was a gory mess of his intestines poking through the hole in his abdomen. In an almost calm voice, Rod said, "I keep shoving them back in, but as soon as I take a step, my guts pop back out."

Moving in closer, I looked at his wound. Not only was there a wide slice in his belly, but his intestines had also been cut. Any bacteria inside the intestines were now roaming freely inside Rod Edwards. Even if we could get him to a hospital in time in Denver, which was over three hours away to get him patched up, the bacteria would more than likely kill him in the end. The wound I was looking at was almost always a fatal one.

Looking around trying to determine the best place to make a stand against those that were behind us, I said, "Well, I guess we make a stand here since you are in no shape to climb the Edwards Sluice." "No, Dane! You need to get Laney and the others to safety. I am going to stay here awhile."

Rod Edwards just showed what a man he truly was, for I knew what he was thinking. "That's not acceptable!"

Rod gathered his strength and stood straight up and looked me in the eye and with pride in his voice, "It is what I was born to do. I trained for this, for I am a Dog Soldier. I have no dog rope today to pin myself to the ground, but this path is my final battle ground. I was a man born out of time, but my heritage has finally caught up with me to give me the chance to honor my ancestors. In my death there will be goodness for Laney and the rest of you so that you can live your lives!"
There was wisdom and strength in Rod Edwards' words, and I knew even in his wounded and fatal condition he would give the rest of us a better chance of coming out of this alive if he slowed down the remaining members of the Insurgence. A sense of remorse flooded over me. "I was wrong about you, Rod. I apologize for that."

WHEN THE SONG VANISHES

Rod grimaced when he reached out and put his hand on my shoulder, and there was a slight chuckle when he spoke, "You were not wrong about me, Dane. Let's be truthful here; I have never fit into today's society. Been an outcast my entire life. I was not meant to live in these modern times. I definitely would never fit into Laney's new life. In the end I would just become an embarrassment to her, and she deserves much more than that. I love Laney McKay more than anything in this world, but for now honor me by not telling her the truth until this is all over. She respects you and Nickey; please make her understand this was the only way."

Rod Edwards was a man of the mountain, a fierce warrior, and a Cheyenne Dog Soldier and with some effort, he buttoned up his coat so not to show his wound when Nickey, John, and Laney stepped onto the trail with Rod and myself. Nickey spoke first, "So what's the plan? We need to keep moving!"

A couple of tears formed in my eyes as I looked straight at Rod as I answered, "Rod has a plan and I have agreed to it. He is going to take one of the Uzi's, 45 Colt pistol, and his Henry rifle and blaze a trail away from the rest of us in the hope that they will follow him."

Nickey saw my tears and heard the quiver in my voice, and she knew I was not telling the truth. Laney hurried over to Rod and in a quiet but angry voice said, "That sounds like a stupid plan to me. Rod, tell me you will not do this!"

Rod pulled Laney in tight and hugged her, whispering in her ear loudly enough that we all could hear, "I love you so much! You are the world to me and there is nothing I would not do to protect you! Trust me, baby, this is the best way. You know of my abilities in the woods: therefore, I am better off alone. I move better when solo and I become one with the woods. This is the only way out of this for all of us. I promise you, when this is all done, I will come to Nashville like you have been asking me to do."

With tears now in Nickey's eyes, she now suspected the truth. Tears also flowed from Laney's eyes as she believed the lie and held on to Rod. "I am going to hold you to that promise, Rod. When this is all over, things will be better for the both of us."

Rod nuzzled Laney away. "We are wasting valuable time. Laney, since you know the sluice better than anyone, you need to continue to lead and show the others the safest route. Now get going!"

Laney, with a sparkle in her eye, gave her lover a long kiss and took to the trail so the rest of us could follow her to the sluice. Nickey hesitated, and I pointed toward Laney. "Deputy Lee, get moving, and you too John!"

Looking at Rod Edwards, there was nothing I could say to ease what was happening. Rod broke the silence, "Dane, I got everything I need. Keep my girl safe; I am counting on you!" Knowing this would be the last time I would see Rod Edwards alive, I reached out and shook his hand and then pulled him in for a hug. Rod responded then said, "Get going, you big lug before people get the wrong impression about us."

With a heavy heart and without looking back, I turned toward the trail and followed the others.

I caught up with Laney, Nickey, and John as Laney took charge of the trail. Once again, I was impressed with Laney's ability in the woods. She was quick and silent as she pushed onward and set a rapid pace. Obviously, she knew this trail well.

I tried to push any thoughts of Rod to the back of my mind, for there was nothing now I could do about the situation with him. I thought of what lay ahead and what needed to be done. The one advantage we had was Laney who knew these woods better than the remaining four members of the Insurgence. They would not know what we were attempting to do about getting to a phone. Nor would they know about the Edwards Sluice. Once we made it to the sluice and gained some altitude by climbing in the dark, they would not be able to see us, and it would be impossible to track us over the granite boulders and rocks. Once they lost our trail at the bottom of the sluice, they may even dismiss the thought of us even attempting to climb such a dangerous avenue with two women. Of course, I could not count on that, but it was a possibility.

The mountain before us was looming close, and I knew we would be at the sluice in a couple of minutes. Stopping and looking behind me, I concentrated on the night sounds of the wilderness trying to hear anything out of the norm. The bodies of the Insurgence compadres and Barry Mason would have been found by now. After a brief spell, they would have been able to locate our trail, for these were seasoned men in the wild. I had no doubt they were heading in our direction. Good news was they must not have caught up to where Rod Edwards was waiting on the trail for them. There had been no gunshots or sounds of battle behind me. Then there was always the possibility that Rod had already succumbed to his wounds and had died before they reached his ambushed point. I didn't even want to ponder that thought.

Turning back toward the front, I ran another thirty yards following the game trail through the dark timber before reaching the others at the bottom of Edwards Sluice.

CHAPTER 14

"Looks daunting and dangerous!" John said.

Laney was not even out of breath, and she replied, "Done this ten or twelve times over the years in the dark. Just follow my path."

Laney wasted no time and started up the incline of Edwards Sluice. She took a few seconds of being sure of her footing before climbing. Once assured, in a few minutes, Laney was about forty feet up the sluice. Looking toward the top in the darkness, I could not see our eventual destination, but I knew it would take us several hours to reach the top. Nodding at Nickey, "You're next *Mi Vida*."

Watching my wife as she started up the incline, being very careful to follow in the same path of Laney, I felt tremendous joy in the woman I loved. She was not only intelligent and beautiful, but she also had spunk. Knowing what she had gone through just over a year ago and here recently with the shoot-out at the bank and watching her take on this dangerous and difficult task of climbing Edwards Sluice brought a swelling of pride to my chest.
I could no longer see Laney and when Nickey was about forty feet up the incline, I said in an almost whisper, "You're next John."

John hesitated and seemed a tad reluctant to begin the climb, but he did. Once he started, I turned and listened to the night sounds and concentrated trying to hear anything that might be a telltale of how close behind those that were hunting the four of us were. In the distance I could hear the hoot of a far-away owl and nothing more. Hearing nothing out of the usual, I waited until John was forty feet up the incline before I slung the Uzi and my rifle over my shoulder and started in my ascent of Edwards Sluice.

I paid close attention to each handhold and foothold that John was using, hoping he had done the same with Nickey as she progressed up the incline. Any misstep or trusting the wrong handhold could cause a fall and tumble over very sharp granite. Any fall could have consequences of serious injuries and possibly death.

Once I was up over forty feet, I breathed a slight sense of relief, knowing that none of us now could be seen in the dark from the bottom of the sluice.

After an hour of climbing and about 100 yards up the sluice, I surmised that I had probably reached the half-way point and that Laney was already at the top or at least very close. I could still see John above me and he had stopped. I assumed Nickey whom I could not see had stopped for a breather, so John had as well. Stopping myself, I breathed in the cool night air and felt it refreshing my lungs. There was no breeze to speak of, and the solitude and the stillness of the night were overpowering.

The moon's arc had moved to the west and from its position, I guessed it was close to four a.m. Hopefully ample enough time to put us at the top of Edwards Sluice while it was still dark. We were not out of danger but hopefully close to a telephone or possibly high enough to get a good signal to transmit on my police band walkie-talkie the twenty-seven miles to our office.

Looking downward first, then over my shoulder in the direction that we had traveled, I saw the flash first of gunfire before the sound reached my ears. Several more seconds passed before the area of the first flash lit up as a full fledge firefight was now being fought as the remaining radicals had stumbled into Rod Edwards' ambush. It would seem that Rod had not succumbed to his wound yet and was making a heroic effort and a last stand to engage our enemy.

Still watching the flashes of gunfire, I knew I would never be able to thank Edwards for this gallant effort to save not only his girlfriend but also Nickey, John, and myself. Rod was definitely a man born out of time with an ancient code of honor. Rod Edwards, the last of the Dog Soldiers, had my ultimate respect.

Looking upwards, I saw John start his climb once more, so I began again. After a full ten minutes of rapid and continuing gunfire, it suddenly stopped, and the silence overpowered the woods. No more flashes in the night showing that Rod Edwards was still alive. There were several minutes of stillness and silence; then there was one more gunshot in the distance. I didn't see it, but I knew in my heart it was a *coup de grâce*, and that Rod Edwards' life was now at an end.

Not knowing if Edwards had been successful knocking down the numbers of the radicals that still hunted us, I suspected now that the remaining members of the Insurgence would be even more cautious in their approach, not knowing if another ambush was in the offering. That would buy us more time…time we needed to make good our escape and bring in the Calvary.

A full hour later I was at the top of Edwards Sluice as John and Nickey each gave me a hand and pulled me over the rim of the sluice. Looking downward in the dark, I could see no one behind me, but I did not know if they were close or had lost our trail. Standing fully erect, I pulled Nickey into my arms to give her some love, before asking, "Did we get a hold of our office yet?" Nickey holding me tight, "Yes, Laney had already called it in on Isabella's telephone. Sheriff Walker is in route with Deputy Zach Lewis. He called the FBI, and they are helicoptering in a special weapons and tactics team out of Denver. The gunshots earlier? Do you think Rod is still alive?"

WHEN THE SONG VANISHES

Looking Nickey in the eyes, I could see she already probably knew the answer. "The reason Rod stayed behind was that he had already received what probably was going to be a fatal wound in the knife fight with the Insurgence radical. I am actually surprised he survived long enough to engage the remaining members. I am sure if he had lived through the gunfight, he has by now fallen victim to the earlier wound. That being the case, we need to make sure that his sacrifice was not in vain. We need to move to the house and join the others. I am not sure how far behind those that kidnapped Laney are, or how soon we will get the help we need to survive the rest of the night!"

Taking one last look down the Edwards Sluice, I didn't see anyone. Gently grabbing Nickey's arm, I hustled her toward the front door of Isabella's cabin.

Inside the cabin were Laney, Isabella, John, and now Nickey and me. Unslinging from my back the Uzi and my M-14 carbine, I handed the carbine and two fresh magazines to John. "If they found our trail, they will be coming up the sluice just as we did. Find a window with a clear line of sight and stay alert."
Nickey didn't even hesitate as she had already found a window with a line of sight to the sluice and had her M-14 carbine at ready. Laney and Isabella were both armed; Isabella was with the same Henry lever action rifle I had seen her with earlier; and Laney was holding a duplicate Henry rifle in her hands, which I just assumed had belonged to Isabella's husband before he died. It would seem that the Edwards family kept Henry Rifles in business all by themselves.

Laney and Isabella stepped forward and Isabella reached out and lay her fingers on my forearm. "My son? Any news of my son?"
Clearing my voice and first looking at Laney's worrisome face, I settled in on Isabella and took a second to gather my thoughts. "Rod, before he decided to stay behind, had been wounded severely. He believed, as did I, that the best chance to get Laney to safety was for him to cover our back trail. An hour or more ago we

could see the flashes and hear the gunfire of a firefight. Your son did what he was born to do, and he took the fight to the enemy as only a Cheyenne Dog Soldier would have the courage to do. There is always a possibility he is still alive. Don't get your hopes up though; even if he had survived the firefight, his previous wound more than likely would prove fatal given the circumstances."

Isabella's face went blank, and she sat down hard on the sofa in her living room. Laney's eyes watered, but she held the tears back as she tried to compose herself. She sat down next to Isabella and held her hand as this new information filtered into her mind. The radio on my belt came with a loud hiss and the sound of static before Sheriff Walker's voice came over it, "Dane, if you can copy this, Laney gave us a quick rundown of your situation on the telephone. I am inbound to your position with Zach and ETA is twenty-five minutes. SWAT out of Denver should be airborne within ten minutes and at your location in ninety minutes. What is your status?"

Pushing the transmit button of the radio, "We have Laney and are forted up at Isabella Edwards' cabin. Counting Laney, there are five of us - John Combs, Isabella Edwards, Nickey, and myself. We have a possibility of four hostiles descending on the cabin. Causalities are a possible count of four. Clarence O'Brien and Bob Jonasen of the Insurgence are dead. Barry Mason is dead and highly possible that Rod Edwards has not survived."

CHAPTER 15

Isabella Edwards was in shock. The entire episode of Laney's kidnapping and the more than probable death of her son had been dropped in her lap in the last several minutes. Her mind was trying to understand the ramifications of it all.

Now that she had a few minutes to actually think about the events of this day, Laney was in disbelief of what was happening. Laney was upset, of course, but seemed more pissed than anything. Given the circumstances, I could not think of any celebrity that would not be balled up in a corner cringing in fear. Laney seemed more than willing to fight back for not only what had happened to her, but also for Barry and of course Rod. Laney, like my Nickey, was a woman to ride the river with. She had strength and endurance, and I had no doubt given the chance she would hurt those that have hurt her and hers.

The radio on my belt hissed and crackled. Then Sheriff Walker's voice broke the silence, "We are ten to twelve minutes out. Your call Dane, do you want us silent or with the sirens blaring?"

"Blaring, and as loud as you can be. Light up the morning with the bubble lights. Hopefully, a show of strength will make these assholes think twice and they back off."

Almost immediately we could hear the sirens of two Grand County Sheriff Blazers in the distance. The morning sky was going through the transformation of night to day, and the ebony was slowly turning dark blue. It had been a long and sleepless night. Looking at the entrance from the road to the house, I knew the Sheriff and Zach would have to drive by the top of the Edwards Sluice. Running this through my brain pan, I was deciding if this was a good thing or not. I knew that the remaining members of the Insurgence would climb up the sluice. Keying my police radio, "Sheriff and Zach, be aware that once you reach the road to the Edwards' cabin, thirty yards up that road on your left is where I expect the hostiles to make their appearance."

There were two quick replies, both saying the same thing, "Understood."

Stepping out onto the front porch of the cabin, I posted up behind the eighteen inch thick lodge pole pine post that held up the overhang and focused on the top of the sluice and the road that drove right by it. The air was crisp, and I could see my breath as I exhaled. The Uzi machine pistol was hanging by the sling off my shoulder, but for now I held my Ruger Blackhawk in my right hand.

As the sky grew lighter with the approaching day, the sirens grew louder as the sheriff and Zach made their way up the dirt road. I did not know if the remaining members were still hunting us or if they had given up the chase after their run in with Rod Edwards. My hope was they had quit, but my gut instinct was telling me that men of the caliber and disposition of the Insurgence would not take it lightly after finding two of their members dead. My thought is they would now look for revenge.

As the sirens got louder, I pondered about the four remaining members and the briefs we had from the FBI on each. Venturing a guess, I thought that the former Green Beret and Master Sergeant Dan Minuex would be their leader. The second in command would be Dan's most trusted ally, and that would be his brother Mitch

WHEN THE SONG VANISHES

Minuex. Boyd Thomas, the former Green Berets Sergeant First Class, and Gary Lewis, the weapons specialist who was a former Master Sergeant of the Green Berets, rounded out those that we were up against. All hailed from the small town of Dighton in Lane County, Kansas. All had an ax to grind against the government. Each man was as dangerous as the next. We had been lucky so far to survive this night; I was hoping our luck would hold out. Sheriff Walker's Chevy Blazer appeared on the road and drove by the top of the sluice on the way to the cabin without incident. The next two things to happen did so almost at the exact time. The second Grand County Sheriff Blazer and a lone shadowy figure appeared at the top of the sluice. Zach's Blazer burst into flames as they peppered it with an Uzi and then a hand grenade. Zach Lewis' body was on fire and was thrown from the wreckage forward, and what was left of him landed in front of the destroyed Blazer. The deputy's body was unmoving. My hope was he had died instantly in the blast and not from the hellfire that was now consuming his body.

Just as the initial blast from the Blazer went from detonation to a full fledge fire of the vehicle, gunfire erupted from the house as Nickey and John let loose with their M-14's. Nickey shouted, "I count four hostiles!"

John added, "Confirmed, I count four as well."

Behind the wreckage, I saw two crouching shadows cross the road to the south behind the burning wreckage, and two stayed behind a rock at the top of the sluice. My count was like the others as I observed four hostiles. It would seem that Rod Edwards had slowed down the radicals so we could make good of our escape but failed to kill any of them.

Sheriff Walker was still seated in his Blazer, looking back at the body of Zach and the wreckage of the Blazer. Standing behind the lodge pole post, I yelled, "Tom, time to move! Nickey, we need some cover fire for Tom."

Sheriff Tom Walker recovered quickly and exited the Blazer with his service pistol at ready and firing in the sluice's direction as John, Nickey, and I opened up at the radicals' last known position giving the sheriff a small window to make it to the porch without getting shot.

Just as the sheriff stepped foot on to the wooden porch, an air concussion hit us as his Grand County Sheriff Blazer exploded as another hand grenade found its mark. Being forted up in a log cabin with thick walls was one thing but being forted up when the opposition had hand grenades was another thing. We were in deep shit, more so than I had ever thought.

Just when I thought it couldn't get worse, the sheriff collapsed and face planted onto the porch. Kicking the front door open, I grabbed the sheriff by his underarms and dragged him inside. Once on the inside, Laney and Isabella helped me drag him further into the room as I slammed the front door shut.

After helping me haul in the sheriff, Laney joined Nickey and John at the windows and starting using the Henry rifle and helped in the barrage toward the sluice.

Kneeling, I asked the sheriff, "Have you been shot?"

Grimacing, the sheriff said, "Not sure."

That is when I saw a piece of six-inch jagged metal sticking out of his left side just above the small of his back. Not wanting to mince words, I said, "Looks as if you took some shrapnel from the explosion."

"How bad is it?"

Taking another quick gander at the metal and wound, "Not going to lie, Tom. Looks bad, there is a six-inch piece of metal hanging outside the penetration. Not sure how much is imbedded inside."

WHEN THE SONG VANISHES

Reaching down, I was going to remove the metal, but Isabella grabbed my hand and shook her head, no. Tom saw the exchange and said, "Isabella is right, do not remove it. It may be the only thing keeping me from bleeding out. It might be plugging any organ or veins in the short term that have been pierced."

Realizing Isabella may have prevented me from killing my friend, I looked her in the eyes and then gently kissed her on the forehead. She responded, "I will tend to him. You have more important matters to attend to, like keeping us all alive."

Knowing the sheriff was in better care with Isabella than myself, keeping low, I half crawled toward Nickey and the window she was defending when all gunfire ceased. Once I got next to Nickey, I sat up and put my back to the log wall. "Nickey, what is our status?"

The sun of the new morning had made its appearance as I took a quick peak out the window and then quickly drew back behind the safety of the wall as Nickey responded to my question, "I still count four. Last I saw, there are two hostiles on the south side of the road, and two on the north side. They quit firing and with no new targets, so did we."

Pondering what I saw and what Nickey's observations were, I knew the only way for us to survive was for the SWAT team to get here in time. Having hand grenades had turned the tide of the battle in the favor of our enemies. The smell of burning rubber and metal was stinging my nose. Remembering what I had seen when I had looked out the window, the burning wreckage of Zach's Blazer had effectively blocked the road in both directions. I pulled my radio from my belt and pressed the transmit button to call dispatch, "Yvonne, are you in contact with the SWAT team helicopter?"

After a brief crackle and hiss of the airway, "They are using channel six."

Before switching to channel six, I said, "Yvonne, Sheriff Walker is wounded and in need of medical evacuation. Call Saint Joe's in Denver and get the biggest Flight for Life helicopter they have in the air. We may have more wounded before they get here. Also get ahold of the Grand County Fire Department; we have two vehicles on fire. Which Grand County deputy is on duty this morning?"

Yvonne responded, "Tina Roberts."

Tina was a thoughtful and resourceful deputy. "Have her set up a roadblock at the entrance of Rocky Mountain National Park and have her stay in contact with the Flight for Life and fire department. Have the helicopter set down at the roadblock and hold up the fire department there as well until we have a better understanding of what is going on. We still have a hostile situation right now."

With a hiss and crackle of the airway, Yvonne responded, "Understood, will have Tina set up a roadblock and have Flight for Life and fire department meet her there waiting for further instructions."

John Combs yelled across the room, "Dane, the fire just jumped from Zach's Blazer into the evergreens!"

CHAPTER 16

Shaking my head in disbelief, I thought to myself, "Perfect, a forest fire, which just rounds out the day."

Keeping low, I looked out the window and just as John had said, the evergreens on both sides of the road were on fire and a mountain wind pushing up from the sluice was flashing the fire in our direction.

The evergreen trees on fire at the moment were directly above the last known whereabouts of the Insurgence members. "Does anyone have a location of the hostiles?"

Nickey answered first and then John, both saying, "Negative."

What a shit show - hand grenades, forest fire, wounded comrades, and now we have lost the location of the enemy. Not once since we entered the forest in search of Laney have we been in control. We had been dealt a poor hand, one right after another and have been forced to react to the deteriorating circumstances as they occurred. I was at a loss on how to reverse that. The only thing going for us at this moment was a helicopter of SWAT members was inbound and the Insurgence members would not know that. Switching to channel six on my police radio, "This is Dane Lee, Undersheriff of Grand County to inbound helicopter. We have wounded, and the situation is deteriorating quickly on the ground. Looking for an ETA. Do you copy?"

Nickey moved closer so we were touching each other, and she lay her hand on mine. "Just like my Cowboy, always knows how to show a girl a good time."

Seeing the twinkle in her eye even at this moment of extreme danger told me once again I had married the right woman. With a slight chuckle, "Keep your boots and panties on *Mi Vida*, I am just getting started."

Nickey's hand tightened on mine, and her eyes turned serious, "I love you, Dane Lee! Would have wanted nothing different, not now, not ever."

It was as if time had stopped and all that mattered in this moment was my love for this woman. Looking her in the eyes, I felt our tenderness, our closeness, our love that some folks only dream of. "I love you Nickey Lynn! I have never wanted for another, not now, not ever."

My police radio came to life with a crackle and a hiss, "This is Special Agent Lon Comstock, Undersheriff Lee, and we copied you. ETA 35 minutes. What is your status?"

"We have been under attack by four hostiles. Hostiles are former Special Forces and are armed with Uzis and hand grenades. Sheriff is severely wounded."

Special Agent Lon Comstock asked, "Do you have colored smoke to pop to determine exact location?"

Sheriff Walker yelled out when Comstock had asked if we had colored smoke, "Tell him we are easy to spot! Just follow the black smoke to the freaking forest fire."

WHEN THE SONG VANISHES

"Negative on color smoke. We have regular smoke. Forest has caught fire, and we are forted up in the cabin on the east side of the fire. Within ten minutes, the cabin will be in the center of the fire. Location at this time of hostiles is unknown."

Smoke was already getting thick inside the cabin when the evergreen right next to the house exploded into a blazing fire, which sent flaming debris on to the roof and front porch of the cabin. John yelled out across the room, "The barn is already on fire, but the garage for now is out of the path of the fire and far enough away from the barn to maybe not catch fire."

I ran this additional information through my thinker as choking black smoke was now barreling through every room in the cabin. I could hear the flames roar as they danced across the roof and the bottom of the eaves, and the front porch was now fully engulfed in flames. We could not survive here in the cabin until the SWAT team arrived. "Folks, we are going to make a run for the garage. John, I need you to help me move the sheriff. Nickey, I need you to secure the back door. Take Laney and Isabella with you."

Nickey armed with her service pistol and M-14 carbine stayed low as she moved swiftly toward the rear of the cabin while Laney and Isabella followed Nickey by staying low beneath the smoke and both carrying their Henry lever action rifles.

John joined me as I spoke to the sheriff. "Tom, we are going to have to drag you outside to stay low under the smoke. We will try not to bump you too hard."

As John and I got a handhold under each of the sheriff's armpits, the sheriff said, "Dane, guess my coming to your rescue didn't go according to plan."

As we started pulling Tom Walker across the floor, I replied, "If we get out of this alive, you owe me a cold Coors Light."

"If I got to drink a Coors Light, leave me here." The sheriff, even in the face of death, was still a Budweiser fan. I saw John roll his eyes to the sheriff's remark and if not for the circumstances of the moment, I would have laughed out loud.

By the time we dragged Tom to the back door, I could see flames rolling across the interior front of the cabin walls. The fire was spreading through the cabin fast devouring the front of it first. Nickey, Laney, and Isabella had all made their exit out the back door and were using an old wagon that Isabella had turned into a flower planter as cover. So far there had been no more gunfire. Could we have gotten so lucky that the Insurgence members had left the scene?

Once we got Tom dragged to the old wagon, I asked Nickey, "What is our status?"

There was a loud crash and flaming embers shot high into the air as the front porch of Isabella's cabin collapsed before Nickey responded, "Nothing, no resistance of any kind. No helicopter, no radicals, a whole bunch of nothing. Do you think those assholes are gone?"

"I hope so but not counting on it. Every time I assume something in the last twenty-four hours, I have been wrong, dead wrong. We are too exposed out here in the open, I want to keep moving toward the garage."

Speaking to everyone now, "We are going to fort up in the garage until the SWAT team gets here."

The sky was full of black and grey smoke from the cabin and forest fire now burning. My nose was stinging from the smell of burnt wood and rubber. As I looked around at all the survivors, I thought we were a sorry-looking lot. All of us were worn, haggard looking, and our clothes were filthy with smoke and ash. It had been a tough twenty-four hours with no sleep.

Our new destination, the stick-built three car garage, was thirty yards to the south. The garage doors were closed, and the man door was in the far southwest corner of the garage - the furthest point away. Just in front of the man door was the 1972 Chevy blue and white two-tone pickup that Nickey and I had seen earlier. The only sound I could hear was the flames roaring behind us. I saw no movement or sign of the radicals in front of us.

Pointing at Tom, but looking at John, "John, going to need some help with the sheriff again."

John and I stood the sheriff up in between us as we walked the sheriff forward. "How you doing, Tom?"

"Legs feel like rubber and my entire body is cold and numb."

Taking it slowly, John and I moved the sheriff forward as I spoke to Tom again, "Help is on the way, my friend. SWAT should be here in no time, and I reckon they will have a medic with them so they can take a look at you."

Moving toward the garage, Nickey had taken point after holstering her pistol. She had her M-14 carbine at the ready. Laney and Isabella were behind her, both still carrying the Henry rifles. John and I were in the rear helping Tom. My radio hissed and Special Agent Comstock's voice came over the airway, "Be advised, Undersheriff Lee, we see black smoke and are heading for it. ETA fifteen minutes. What is your status?"

Stopping long enough to speak on the radio, "We had to abandon the cabin because it caught fire. We are moving to the three-car garage directly south of the cabin. We are exposed, but no sign of hostiles."

"Copy that."
Reaching the tailgate of the Chevy pickup, I was feeling a sense of relief. But on this day, that sense of relief was short-lived. I did not

hear the report of the gun that fired the bullet that struck John Combs in the face and burst half of his head into a red lingering mist until long after John had dropped to the ground dead. Losing the support that John had been providing to help prop up the sheriff, Tom and I both stumbled first, then went down…hard. Rolling to my right, I fumbled to draw my Ruger pistol. The roll brought me to my knees with my pistol drawn just as Dan Minuex knocked Isabella to the ground and then grabbed Laney by her long hair, yanking her toward him, making her drop her rifle. I squeezed one shot off in the leader's direction; I missed but hit Gary Lewis in the center of his exposed throat. Lewis had been standing next to Dan as he struggled to control Laney who was fighting the radical like an alley cat. Gary Lewis slumped to the ground…unmoving.

Even in the heat of battle and the desperate struggle for all of us to live, I could hear the recent gunshots ringing in my ears and the helicopter as it hovered overhead.

Isabella Edwards was fighting her own battle as she fought with Boyd Thomas. Thomas started to get the advantage when he slapped her several times. With Dan Minuex occupied trying to control Laney, I swung my pistol to line up a shot on Boyd Thomas. The next minute moved through my mind in slow motion as several factors and events took place all at the same time.

Dan Minuex finally had enough of trying to subdue Laney, and he uppercut her with his right hand, sending her sprawling to the ground. One of the SWAT members from the hovering helicopter fired and sent a round through the head of Boyd Thomas as he attacked Nickey before I could line up for a shot. At the exact second the SWAT team member killed Boyd Thomas, Mitch Minuex kicked my pistol out of my hand and then stepped back and smiled as he leveled his Colt 45 automatic at my head just as the SWAT team members repelled out of their helicopter and had boots on the ground.

Mitch Minuex squeezed the trigger of his Colt several seconds after Laney, lying on the ground, had regained her rifle and levered a shell and fired on instinct right through Mitch Minuex's throat. Mitch staggered and tried to raise his pistol again. Laney wasn't having any of that and levered another shell into the chamber, and she shot him again - this time just below his nose. Mitch Minuex's body slumped to the ground dead.

As the SWAT team converged on our position, I realized everyone was accounted for except Dan Minuex. The elder Minuex most have faded into the tree line south of the Garage.

CHAPTER 17

I tried to stand but stumbled and fell hard again to the ground. It was not until I had tried to stand that I realized Mitch had shot me. My side was now hurting something fierce and placing my right hand above my hip, it came away bloody. Laney's well-placed bullet had made Mitch Minuex, who had been aiming at my head, falter his shot placement and instead of a killing shot in my noggin, he had placed one into my right side just above my hip. Reaching behind me, I could feel the exit wound. Not a fatal wound, and more than likely no vitals had been punctured. The one thing I knew was that Laney McKay had saved my life when she had killed the radical.

Turning my head, I saw Laney had gathered Isabella into her arms, and they both looked shell-shocked. Laney looked at me, and I gave her a nod of my head in a silent thank you for saving my life. She returned the nod as a tear formed in her eye. I knew from my own encounters in the past that Laney McKay would – for a long time - not get over what happened today with the death of Rod and her taking a human life. Taking a man's life and everything that he would ever be is a powerful soul searching experience. Some folks in time learn to move on from it; others straddle the fence of the sane and the insane because of it. Time will only tell how Laney comes out of this.

WHEN THE SONG VANISHES

Nickey had seen me fall, and she rushed to my side. "Dane, are you okay?"

Looking into my lover's face and the concern she showed brought everything that had happened today into realization. I reached up with my bloody hand and placed it behind her head and brought her in close to hug her. Nickey Lynn - *Mi Vida* - was my reason for living. We were lucky to be alive. Answering her, "Well, sort of, that son of a bitch shot me. I do not believe it will slow me down much though."

The entire scene was surreal. A warming sun was shining in a cloudless sky but being blacked out from time to time as the smoke from the forest fire wafted over it, creating deep dark shadows that flowed over the landscape like ghostly specters. An updraft of wind from the sluice was now taking the fire away from us and pushing it north, which was the only thing we had going for us now. The sound "chuff, chuff, and chuff" was oscillating from the hovering helicopter blades. It seemed as if everything that was happening was in slow motion.

One of the SWAT team was looking to the needs of Laney and Isabella. Two members of the SWAT team had removed the weapons from the dead radicals and began securing the site. One SWAT medic and another team member were tending to the sheriff and were loading Tom into a rescue "stokes basket" as the helicopter hovering above dropped some lines to tie off the basket. They were getting ready to lift Tom down to where the Flight for Life helicopter had landed at the entrance to the park so they could get him to Saint Joe's hospital in Denver.

A SWAT team member took off his helmet and squatted down next to Nickey and me. He lifted my shirt and examined my wound. "Undersheriff Dane Lee, I presume. My name is Special Agent Lon Comstock, and we spoke briefly on the radio. I have seen worse wounds and I think you will live. Soon as we get the sheriff secured and on the Flight for Life, we will fly you down to the entrance of the park. I understand there is an ambulance and paramedics there and they can look at you. In the meantime, do you feel well enough to give a status report?"

Looking at the rescue basket as it started to lift off, "How is the sheriff?"

"Not going to lie, it is a serious wound, but he has pain in his legs, which is a good thing. Currently, we do not know how much internal damage is done. We will get him to the Flight for Life and get him in the air as soon as possible. He seems to be in good spirits, and he mentioned to me that if you bring up anything about buying him a Coors Light that I was supposed to shoot you. I promised him I would."

Nickey, Special Agent Comstock, and I all laughed at that. "Well, Special Agent Comstock, it has been one hell of a night. By my count there are nine dead - three deputies John Combs, Zach Lewis, and Barry Mason; One civilian named Rod Edwards; and five of the Insurgence radicals - Bob Jonasen, Clarence O'Brien, Gary Lewis, Boyd Thomas, and Mitch Minuex. The leader of the Insurgence Dan Minuex and probably the most dangerous one faded into the woods south of here when you shot the one radical from the helicopter. He is armed with an Uzi, an automatic Colt 45, and possibly hand grenades."

Special Agent Comstock stood straight up and keyed his radio, "We have one hostile not accounted for named Dan Minuex. Suspect is former Special Forces and is armed and dangerous with possible hand grenades, an Uzi, and a Colt 45. Last seen twenty minutes ago south of my position."

Several minutes ticked by, and Comstock's radio came alive, "We have vehicles inbound for your extraction. Forest fire is riding the breeze and moving north, but Command is worried that may not hold up for long. Command wants everyone on the ground, including civilians and all SWAT members, to rendezvous at the Rocky Mountain National Park entrance. Special Agent Ken

WHEN THE SONG VANISHES

Ekross is setting up a command post there. Aerial firefighting tankers are inbound from Colorado Springs. Command wants no one in the field until the fire is under control. Repeat everyone on the ground needs to rendezvous at command post."

The SWAT helicopter's "chuff, chuff, and chuff" could be heard as it came in low over the evergreens to the south after dropping the sheriff off. It lowered the rescue stokes basket so I could follow Tom down the mountain. As Nickey and Special Agent Comstock fussed over me as they strapped me in the basket, I felt foolish and embarrassed. Looking at my wife, "Can't I just ride down with you? I don't need this damn contraption."

Nickey laughed, "Look at it as a onetime ride that hopefully you never have to make again. Just don't toss your lunch like you did on the Tilt-a-Whirl at Elitch Gardens last summer."

Smiling at the memory, "I had an excuse, I was a little drunk." As the helicopter started to take off, so did the rescue basket and the last thing I heard was Nickey saying with a laugh, "You were more than a little drunk, mister."

The basket spun twice before we started the descent down the mountain over the top of the evergreens, giving me a full 360 view of the forest fire that was now raging north of us. The black smoke and ash filled the air, and the smell of burnt wood and evergreen needles was burning in my throat and nose. As we got closer to the entrance of the park where the command post was set up, I could see the white Flight for Life helicopter with the Red Cross lift off as it turned east and picked up speed and headed for Denver. Knowing that it was carrying my boss and friend, I said a silent prayer for him.

The SWAT helicopter hovered straight above me as they lowered the basket and me gently into the outstretched arms of the Grand County paramedics and firefighters. They quickly undid the tethers that bound me to the helicopter and with hand signals showed that

I was free, and then the SWAT helicopter departed back up the mountain.

Once I was inside the ambulance, the paramedics went to work on me to plug the hole in my side that Mitch Minuex had put in me and then got me ready for transport to the small Grand County hospital just outside of Granby.

Just as they were getting ready to close the doors of the ambulance, Special Inspector Ken Ekross stuck his hand in to stop them. Once they fully opened the doors, Ken stuck his head in. "I know you are hurting, Undersheriff Lee, but as soon as they get you to the hospital, we are going to have to do a complete debrief. Just answer one quick question. Is Dan Minuex the only surviving member of the Insurgence?"

"Yes, he is, Ken. He faded into the tree line south of the fire. Not only did he lose five of his team, but Laney McKay was the one that shot and killed his brother Mitch as he was getting ready to shoot me in the head. She fired before he did, and the result is he is dead, and I got one through the side. Dan Minuex saw it all happen. He will not be happy that a celebrity killed his brother. I am sure he will look to avenge the death of his team members and his brother!

CHAPTER 18

After I reached the small hospital in Granby, the staff there was diligent and caring and basically did nothing more than clean my wound and add new bandages, telling me that the paramedics had done a wonderful job. Once the nurse and doctor had left my room, I felt exhausted as the adrenaline rush of the last twenty-four hours seeped away; then the lack of sleep hit me like a sledgehammer. Leaving the television off, I then turned on the small AM/FM radio that was on the bedside table. An old song I remembered well came over the airways that had been released on the Beatles White Album – "I'm So Tired".

I'm so tired, I haven't slept a wink
I'm so tired, my mind is on the blink

As my mind drifted listening to John Lennon sing his tune, I thought of Tom down in the hospital in Denver and then thought of Nickey and wondered if she was okay as sleep finally took me away.

The dream woke me up, not in a panic, but nevertheless woke me up. Opening my eyes, I turned my head and Nickey was kicked back and sound asleep in a recliner that someone had wheeled into my room after I had gone to sleep. Night had fallen and the only light that filled the room came from the partially opened door to the hospital corridor. Watching my wife sleep even to this day always pleased me. She was breathing easily even though I could tell by her clothes she had not been home yet and had come straight to the hospital. I loved this woman like no other. Knowing she was here and safe, I tried to recall the dream.

I huddled down into my sheepskin coat to stay warm as I followed the ghost of my grandfather down a backwoods trail that zigzagged through the evergreens. The wind was pitching a fit as the evergreen needles and tree branches swayed in the cold northern gust. It was night, and a full moon that filtered through the treetops provided the only light to see by. Grandfather was in no hurry as I stayed behind him wondering where we were headed. Every few minutes he would look over his shoulder back at me as his long white as snow hair glistened in the wind with the glow of the moonlight. Several ebony crows flew directly overhead as they announced their presence with a loud, piercing, "caw, caw." Grandfather finally stepped into a clearing, and he walked into the middle, stopped, and turned to face me. Grandfather then looked up into the night sky and so did I as the crows begin to fly in a circle above the clearing with the moon now providing ample light to see by. It baffled me why we were here. I was confused and wondered what the meaning of this dream was. My gaze fell upon my grandfather as he drew his Bowie knife from a fringed buckskin sheath that was at his side. The blade now shimmered and reflected the moon's rays as they danced across the sharp edge. Grandfather now took the knife and pointed behind me. Turning slowly, he pointed to where there were now nine bodies wrapped in blood-spattered sheets on the ground when there had been none before. A cold, icy wind was blowing hard enough that the sheets rippled like the waves on a high mountain lake. The wind, as if orchestrated by that of an unknown maestro, blew the bloody sheets off one by one to expose the nine corpses. The dead that lay on the stony ground were the bodies of John Combs, Rod Edwards, Zach Lewis, Barry Mason, Bob Jonasen, Clarence O'Brien, Gary Lewis, Boyd Thomas, and Mitch Minuex. Looking at the death faces, I knew that each one would haunt my dreams until the day I died. Grandfather stepped up closer to me and gently lay his hand on my shoulder as he spoke in a deep voice, "Nickey and you did well to survive against a great enemy. Many of friend and foe died in a great battle to save the girl. Fate has only given you part of your destiny, for the battle is not over. Heed my words Dane, the one that got away is not done with you or the ones you love. The one of French descent will hide, wait, and strike when you least expect it. My words to you, my grandson, are to take the battle to him where he least expects it. Take the war to where he lays his head at night." I turned to look at grandfather to ask for a better explanation, but Grandfather Matt Lee was no longer there, just the cold, icy wind of the night.

Running the dream through my thinker a couple of times to clear my mind, I realized, unlike all the previous dreams of grandfather, the message was simple in this dream. He was telling me to take the fight to Dan Minuex. I was not so sure that was even going to happen or if I needed to. Right now, Dan Minuex had bigger issues to deal with than the Undersheriff of Grand County coming for his hide. He was on the run in the Rocky Mountains evading capture of not only the FBI, but also that of every country loving redneck in the United States. If it has not happened already, once word gets out that he and his cohorts had kidnapped America's sweetheart, Laney McKay, every American that could read or watch television would be on the lookout for the last remaining member of the Insurgence. Yes, Dan Minuex would be running for his life. Turning to look at Nickey again, I saw her looking at me with a sleepy smile on her face. "You look in deep thought there, Mister Dane."

Smiling at her, "You need to go home and clean up and sleep in a comfortable bed, *Mi Vida*."

"I wanted to be here when you woke up."

"I am awake now, baby!"

Nickey got up and scooted the recliner closer to my hospital bed. Once she got comfy again in the chair, she reached out and grabbed my hand. "You may be awake, but I am not. I am so tired. Let's have this conversation when the sun is actually awake."

As Nickey closed her eyes, she whispered, "I love you, Dane." By the time I replied with, "I love you Nickey," she had already fallen back to sleep.

Holding Nickey Lynn's hand, I was overcome with emotion, and tears welled in my eyes. I loved her so much that just holding her hand brought back a raging flood of memories of what she had gone through in the last year - her face mutilation and near death from the likes of Samael Amos, and now this experience with the members of the Insurgence. For pity's sake, we live in Grand County, Colorado! Things like this just are not supposed to happen here!

Thinking back on the dream and the warning and the advice from my grandfather, I knew he was right. Dan Minuex, if he survived the massive manhunt that I was sure was under way, then he would not back off. He was still a warrior with a cause. The death of his brother and the others of the Insurgence would not slow him down. If anything, it will only strengthen his resolve to act. Everything that had happened would only bolster his radical view of the government that should be overthrown. The death of his fellow team members would only give him martyrs in his quest. The death of his younger brother would give him a thirst for revenge.
As my mind cleared of the sleep fog, I concentrated more on what I would do if I was Dan Minuex. I had no doubt now that the four survivors of the encounter with the Insurgence were in grave danger. Laney, Nickey, I, and even Isabella Edwards were at risk for vengeance and retribution at the hands of Minuex. Laney especially since she had been the one who had killed Mitch Minuex, and Dan knew she was the one, for he had seen it. Just like grandfather said, "Heed my words Dane, the one that got away is not done with you or the ones you love."

WHEN THE SONG VANISHES

My gut instinct was now telling me that whatever happens regarding Dan Minuex would be for me to do. My dreams and grandfather have always proven in the end to be true.

Remembering the words, *"The one of French descent will hide, wait, and strike when you least expect it. My words to you, my grandson, are to take the battle to him where he least expects it. Take the war to where he lays his head at night."*

Squeezing *Mi Vida's* hand a little tighter, I turned to look at her and closed my eyes. Shutting off the dreams and the insights that were swimming in my thoughts, I finally went back to sleep.

CHAPTER 19

The nurse woke me up as she cleaned and bandaged my wound again. The pain of her touching and probing sent spasms all the way up my back and into my shoulders. Wincing, I realized having the pain was much better than the alternative. As I looked about the room for Nickey, the nurse handed me a folded sheet of white paper and then said, "Your wife left several hours ago and left this note for you."

Unfolding the note, it said, "Went home to clean up and then go into the office. Since Tom and you are both out, I am the senior deputy, and someone has to keep Grand County safe until you both can return. Love you, cowboy."

Looking out the window, I saw that the sun was shining, but the sky was full of big puffy clouds. Looking at the distant mountains, I could see the evergreen trees in the distance swaying in the wind. The nurse finished up, and I asked, "Am I going to live?"

She smiled, "I think so. As for getting shot, this one is about as good as it gets. But I would suggest maybe you should start looking for another line of work. Next time you might not get so lucky."

She had a point. That was for sure! "Do you know if there has been an update on Sheriff Tom Walker? They flew him to Denver by Flight for Life."

"I know he survived the surgery and is in intensive care. I will see if I can get more news for you."

"Thank you, and much appreciated. Could you turn on the television and find a news channel?"

As the nurse turned on the television, she said, "The hunt for Dan Minuex was all over the news on every channel. Channel 7 KMGH-TV is doing live updates from Rocky Mountain National Park."

As the picture on the tube came to life, John Lindsey the anchor for Channel 7 appeared. "The forest fire that swept through the area is now fully contained after destroying nearly 4000 acres of woodland thanks to the water bombers out of Colorado Springs. Officials have recovered the bodies of the nine dead as the investigation of exactly what happened continues. Grand County sheriff Tom Walker is in intensive care at Saint Joe's in Denver. Undersheriff Dane Lee is just down the road in the hospital in Granby after being shot and is in recovery. Country singer Laney McKay and a woman named Isabella Edwards are being guarded in an undisclosed location. The man hunt for kidnapping, robbery, and murder suspect Dan Minuex has now intensified since the Colorado National Guard have been brought in to help the FBI in their search for the elusive remaining member of the Insurgence. For those that might not know, Rocky Mountain National Park is 415 square miles of some of the most remote wilderness areas in the world. The search will also extend into the 396 square miles of US forest service land that surrounds the park. Channel 7 is also tracking a severe storm with freezing rain mixed with snow that is to hit this area in the next 48 to 72 hours that may hamper search efforts."

Walking into my room, Special Agent Ken Ekross stated the obvious, "You look like shit."

That made me chuckle as I replied, "It's kind of hilarious watching you try to fit your entire vocabulary into one sentence."

It was Ken's turn to chuckle as he walked over to the television propped up high on the wall. He turned the sound down as an image of two military helicopters flew over the heads of the television crew. Ken then pulled up a chair close to the bed and sat down. The lead investigator for the FBI looked worn and haggard. Noticing the dark circles under his eyes, I said, "Hell Ken, thinking I look better than you."

"Believe me, Undersheriff Lee, I feel just like I look. Just got done taking a statement from Nickey."

Handing me the report he said, "Read this and if it is how you remember it, we do not need to go through the formality of your saying the exact same thing. If you have anything else to add, let me know, and we will add it to the report. Her recollection is that you and the Edwards kid saved lives, especially Laney McKay's life."

Reading the report that Nickey had written, it was precise and a well thought-out retelling of the events that transpired after the Insurgence had kidnapped Laney McKay. Handing the report back to the FBI agent, I said, "I agree with everything in this report expect one thing. Rod Edwards' heroics had more to do with Isabella, Laney, Nickey, and I surviving than any actions I took. Looking back on it, I only reacted to situations and never got ahead of that. I might have made some poor calls along the way. I need to think more on that, but basically the report is accurate."
"Don't beat yourself up too much Dane with over thinking about what would have, should have, and could have happened. The Grand County Sheriff's Department has nothing to be ashamed of

here. You encountered a group of highly trained Special Forces members and disrupted their agenda and killed all but one of their members. That alone is utterly amazing."

Looking Ken straight in the eye, "We lost some good people as well. Their faces will haunt me for the rest of my life."

"I get it, Dane, I truly do. Philosopher Edmund Burke once said, 'The only thing necessary for the triumph of evil is for good men to do nothing.' The good guys need to step up and do what needs to be done; unfortunately, sometimes in this line of work, the good guys die. This incident is one time when good triumphed over evil. Those that died, did not die in vain. You and your people did the right thing."

Still looking Ken in the eye, "It still does not feel like a victory."

The room was quiet for several minutes as the gravity and seriousness of what happened in the wilderness sank into both of us. Ken broke the silence, "You might find it interesting that the company that owns the helicopter that you found tucked away in the trees is sending up a couple of mechanics and a pilot today to check it out mechanically and then hopefully fly it out of here. They are happy to get it back; my guess is those helicopters are not cheap."

I continued to look out the window as several more minutes passed until Ken spoke again, "I want to run something by you and see what you think. My department in the FBI has these shrinks that study criminal behavior and such, and they have come up with this theory about Dan Minuex. These eggheads have decided that it will devastate a man such as Minuex in the aftermath of losing his team and especially his brother. That Minuex sees his rebellion and overthrow of the United States government have failed and would not want to be put on display in any federal courtroom so the lawyers can twist his visions of the world into something that is not righteous. In the aftermath of being bested by a small county sheriff's department - if he has not already done it - he will take his own life. I am curious what a man who has faced Dan Minuex twice might think he would do. Do you think it is possible that he would commit suicide?"

Remembering my grandfather's words from the dream, *"Heed my words Dane, the one that got away is not done with you or the ones you love."*

Shaking my head in disbelief and I am sure rolling my eyes, I replied to Ken's question, "Those behavioral scientists that the FBI employ seem to have no real-world experience, and they have been wrong before. My take on it is that a man such as Dan Minuex, if he is not captured or killed in short order and somehow makes good his escape, will want one thing - revenge. What he is currently experiencing and what happened in the last forty-eight hours will only galvanize his belief that what he is doing is righteous. My best guess, Ken, is that all those members in the Insurgence came up with some bullshit oath that they swore to. I assure you, Ken, that at the end of that oath it was understood they would die trying to fulfill that pledge. Dan Minuex will see those five dead members of the Insurgence as martyrs to that oath and to their rebellion. If he escapes, what happened yesterday and the night before will now become a feud - a blood feud. He will seek revenge and vengeance on that small county sheriff's department that got lucky and bested his unit. Dan Minuex is not a stupid man by any means and is not basing all his reactions on pure emotion. He will not come running down the corridor of this hospital like some wild animal looking to tear me apart. He is a patient hunter and will bide his time until he has the opportune time to strike but believe me, Special Agent Ekross, my wife's life, my life, Isabella Edwards' life, and Laney McKay's life are in extreme danger if he escapes the manhunt. My thought is he will go after Laney first since she was the one who killed his brother."

Ken let what I said soak in for a full minute before speaking, "I agree 100% with you, Dane, and I told those dipshit behavioral guys this very thing last night. Of course, they got all those fancy degrees in psychotic disorder, and my thoughts do not mean diddly squat. I am curious about one thing you said, 'They had been wrong before.' What did you mean by that?"

I was on a roll, and I blurted out without thinking, "Last year when they said the same thing about Samael Amos."

Ken's face went blank as he rolled that around in his thoughts for a minute. "Samael Amos? You mean Samael Amos, the serial killer? The same Amos that almost killed Nickey and cut her face?"

That was a mistake saying that. Looking the Special Agent in the eyes and not wavering, I said nothing more. I was the only one who knew the truth of what happened in the death of Samael Amos. Sheriff Walker and Nickey suspected, of course, but I never told them. During the initial investigation, the sheriff questioned me once but never brought it up again. It was my personal demon that I had to deal with and no one else. The look now on Ken's face told me he now suspected something else other than what was in the official reports of what had happened with Amos.

A smile crept across Ken's face, and he leaned forward in his chair, "Before meeting Nickey and you, and on the way to Grand Lake, I had skimmed a summary about the case of Samael Amos. After meeting Nickey and yourself right after the bank robbery in Grand Lake, I was curious about the both of you, and I wanted to know more. So later on, I pulled all the files the FBI had on what happened here last year regarding Nickey, and you, and Samael Amos. You are absolutely correct. The behavioral guys suggested Amos would also commit suicide, but when his remains had been found, there was not enough left of his corpse to determine cause of death. Now you say they were wrong in that assumption. I can't help but ask myself how you would know that? The reports also said while Nickey was recovering from her wounds and Amos was still unaccounted for that you took an extended leave of absence and rode horseback into Rocky Mountain National Park…in the dead of winter…all alone. When I read that, several questions crossed my mind. Why would a man do that? Did he stumble across a clue where Amos was hiding? Was it a quest for solitude, or was it a quest for vengeance and revenge? Dane, I do not expect answers to these questions. The Samael Amos case is officially closed, and the bad guy is dead. In that case, righteousness won over evil. However, Amos died, I am okay with it. The only other thing I am going to add, Undersheriff Lee, is that I am glad you are one of the good guys and you are on my side. Getting the feeling that beneath that lawman exterior that an ancient warrior's heart beats within your chest. I would hate to run across you when you had vengeance or revenge on your mind. That given the right circumstance, you would disregard the rules and the procedures of modern law and follow that warrior path. Actually, Undersheriff Lee, I admire that. In the old west they would say you have grit...true grit! You are a very interesting fellow, Dane Lee!"

CHAPTER 20

After spending the next two days in the hospital, my body was responding, and I started to heal with no signs of infection.

Speaking with Tom on the phone, he sounded rough, but he told me he was on the mend even though he was still in intensive care. As it turned out, the shrapnel from the Blazer explosion had partially severed an artery and if I had removed it, Tom would have bled out within minutes. Thankfully, Isabella stayed my hand and stopped me from doing just that. Tom and I both had guardian angels that were looking over us on that day.

Nickey was in and out of the hospital to see me but could never stay long since she was running the department in Tom's and my absence. There was a lot for the Grand County Sheriff's Department to do just to go about its own day-to-day operations. The death of three officers also left the department shorthanded. Having the FBI and the National Guard and all their support personnel in the county was also a daunting task for the department. Couple that with the fact that the kidnap and rescue of America's number one country singer Laney McKay was not only national news, but also there apparently were several news channels from other countries following the manhunt for the fugitive Dan Minuex. Once again, the world's spotlight was shining on Grand County.

Every day there were three or four requests for me to do an interview, but I declined them all. I was not in the mood to deal with pandering and accusatory reporters. I felt sort of guilty because Nickey was having to give a daily briefing to the news media since, for the time being, she was in charge of the department. Every time I saw her on the television, she did an outstanding job of keeping everyone up to date and answering the questions posed by the news outlets.

Laney had gone into a guarded seclusion and had taken Isabella Edwards with her. I knew it was probably the best for them both so they could grieve together over the death of Rod Edwards. For myself the death faces of Rod, Barry, Zach, and John invaded my dreams each night. Until the day I die, doubts of my actions on that fateful night will haunt me. Maybe in time I will not second guess myself or wonder what I could have done differently so that all four of those brave souls might have made it out alive after the battle with the Insurgence.

Grandfather had not appeared in my dreams since the first night they admitted me into the hospital, but the visions and his words from that dream were imprinted into my memory. *"Heed my words Dane, the one that got away is not done with you or the ones you love."* I knew deep down inside there was another reckoning to be dealt with; I just didn't know when or where.

Each day I watched John Lindsey, the anchor for Channel 7 news, for updates on the manhunt for Dan Minuex. Each day added a little more frustration as the elusive radical had seemed to have vanished into the mountain mist. Among the FBI, SWAT, and the National Guard, there were over 1000 men in the field looking for any sign of the wanted fugitive. The storm that had been bearing down on the area from the north was almost here and would create even a bigger advantage for Minuex to elude capture.

WHEN THE SONG VANISHES

Watching the manhunt unfold on the news seemed almost dreamlike until I got to thinking it was not the first time Dan Minuex had evaded the law here in the Rocky Mountains. All six of the members had evaded capture right after the bank robbery in Grand Lake while they waited until they could kidnap Laney. At the time of the theft, everyone assumed we were dealing with only two of the six members of the Insurgence, and they had escaped and evaded capture by flying out in a helicopter. I now know that all six members had hid out somewhere close to Grand Lake, but where? The thought formed in my mind that the only explanation why more than 1000 men could not find any trace of the man is that he was not on the run. He had a hidey-hole some place, much the same as Samael Amos had just a year ago. Minuex was holed up somewhere waiting for the manhunt to be called off. I would have to look at Minuex's escape from Isabella Edwards' cabin from a fresh perspective now. The radical had never been on the run. He had to be hiding in plain sight.

Nickey picked me up at 10:00 a.m. on Saturday after I got released from the hospital. My body was healing just fine, but my mind had been adrift for the last several days pondering the disappearance of Minuex. I was now more convinced than ever that the Insurgence radical was holed up some place close to the trailhead where I found their escape helicopter. I was familiar with the area, but the man who really could have helped with this was dead. Rod Edwards would have been the go-to guy if he had been still alive. Once I get home, I was going to have to pull out some of my topographical maps of the area and study them. Nickey was glancing at me as she drove out of the parking lot of the hospital. "Don't shut me out, Dane. Tell me what is going on in that beady little brain of yours. You have been as quiet as a church mouse since I jammed you into the Blazer."

Turning my head to look at my wife, I was struck by how beautiful she looked today. Thinking about what she had said, "Sorry, *Mi Vida*, just lost in thought. Been pondering some on how one man can elude a 1000 man search for him. The only answer I can come up with is that he pulled a Samael Amos."

Nickey's face went blank as she processed what I had just said. Instinctively, she reached up and touched the scar on her face that Amos had left when he tried to kill her. Then her eyes showed understanding. "You think Minuex is hiding out in one spot - that he has never been on the run?"

"Bingo! It must be the same place that all six hid out as they waited for the right time to kidnap Laney. When I get home, I am going to go over some of my old topographical maps. Makes sense to me that he is hiding close to North Supply Creek where I found the helicopter."

Just as Nickey reached the edge of Granby, I saw a woman walking and a boy about ten year's old riding a bike on the side of the road. It was a blue and yellow Schwinn stingray bike with a banana seat and a high sissy bar. Pointing at the woman and the boy, "Pull up there by that woman and stop in front of her. This was a case I was working on the day Laney had been kidnapped. Do you know the woman's or the boy's names?"

Nickey looked confused as she pulled over and stopped in front of the woman, "Yes, that is Joyce Rawlings and her son Joey."

Stepping gingerly out of the passenger seat, I said to Nickey, "Open up the back of the Blazer; I got to steal something back."

Joyce Rawlings and Joey nervously stopped as I approached them. "Ms. Rawlings, do you know who I am?"

"Yes, of course Undersheriff Lee, you have been all over the news the last week. I am confused why you stopped us though."

Joyce seemed hesitant, but she also seemed cooperative. "Well, Ms. Rawlings, it is about some stolen property. Specifically, a bike, to be more precise, a blue and yellow Schwinn stingray bike with a banana seat and a high sissy bar just like the one your son is riding. It would seem that a bike matching that exact description was stolen from a boy named Rusty Himes in Kremmling."

Bending now at the knees, I lowered myself and looked Joey straight in the eyes, and he didn't even flinch. The little shit was scared all right, but he had nerve. I had to give him credit for that. "Going to ask you just once Joey, and keep in mind I am not in a good mood since I was shot this week. Is this your bike?"

Joey at first looked confused, and then he blinked twice as the realization of what was happening was coming full circle. I am sure even a lie or two filtered through his brain, but he finally gave that up and told the truth. "This is not my bike; I stole it in Kremmling."

That took courage for young Joey. As soon as the words rolled out of his mouth, his mom spoke up, "Officer Lee, this is not Joey's fault. It is all my fault. Joey is just trying to protect me; I stole the bike. Joey wanted a bike so bad, and he had never had one. I didn't have the money to buy one, so I borrowed my sister's car and drove to Kremmling and took the first bike I could."

I thought it was far enough away that no one would ever know I took the bike. Joey never knew it was stolen until just now. I told him it was a gift."

Now I knew where Joey got his courage. Joyce was on the verge of crying and her eyes were red, but she was holding her own. Once again, I bent down and looked Joey straight in the eyes and asked, "Now that you know the entire story, what do you think we should do?"

Joey stepped off the bike and he pushed it toward me and said, "It is a good bike and the kid that owns it must be heartbroken. Can you take it back to him, Officer Lee?"
Reaching out, I patted the young man on his shoulder just before I took possession of the bike. "That I can do, Joey."

Nickey silently walked over and the look she gave me was heart breaking as she took the bike from me and rolled it to the back of the Grand County Blazer and put it in the back. Standing back up, I asked Joyce Rawlings if she had any identification. Taking out a pad and pen from my pocket, I wrote her address and all the other information from her driver's license and she almost in a whisper gave me her phone number. Joey and his mom both looked devastated as she asked, "How much trouble am I in, Officer Lee?"

"As of this moment, I am going to consider this a closed case, Ms. Rawlings. You are free to go."

Joyce Rawlings' knees buckled, and the tears rolled, "Thank you Officer, I promise nothing like this will ever happen again. I promise."

Once Nickey and I were both back in the Blazer, Nickey with a look of sadness said, "Sometimes being an officer of the law sucks! Where to now, Dane?"

"We got a stolen bike to return to the rightful owner in Kremmling. No time like the present to get that done."

A little over a half-hour later, we dropped off the blue and yellow Schwinn stingray bike with a banana seat and a high sissy bar to the rightful owner, Rusty Himes who burst into tears once he had his bike back. One boy was happy that he had his bike while another was sad that he just lost his. Nickey was right - sometimes this job sucks.

Nickey was still driving as we headed back to Granby. I was quiet and thinking of the young boys Joey Rawlings and Rusty Himes when the Paul Anka song "Times of Your Life" came over the radio.

The laughter and the tears, the shadows of misty yesteryears,

WHEN THE SONG VANISHES

A thought crossed my mind, and I looked at my wife. "I need you to stop at the hardware store in Granby when we get back in town."

Nickey laughed, "With all that is going on, you are going to start doing that 'honey do' list that I have been harping about for the last six months?"

Smiling, I said, "Maybe! There is something I need to do before I can get my mind focused on Dan Minuex and his disappearance."

Pulling up into the parking lot of the Granby Hardware store, Nickey asked, "Do you need me to come in with you?"

Laughing as I got out of the Blazer, I said, "Nope, you keep your pretty little butt planted. This will not take more than a couple of minutes."

Being a small town, the selection was limited, but I was able to find exactly what I was looking for. After writing a check, I wheeled the new purchase out the door. Once Nickey saw the brand new red and white Schwinn stingray bike with a black banana seat and a high sissy bar, her face split into a huge grin.

Getting out of the Blazer, she helped me load Joey Rawlings' new bike into the back. Shutting the tailgate, she pulled me in close and then with her hand behind my head she pulled me down and kissed me the way that lovers do. After slowly backing away, she looked me in the eye and said, "You are the most wonderful man in the world, Dane Lee! I love you like no other."

"Not sure about being wonderful, *Mi Vida*; it just seemed like the right thing to do. We need to brighten a little kid's day, so let's go drop off Joey's bike to him."

CHAPTER 21

On Sunday the autumn storm blew in from the north with a vengeance. Not rain mixed with snow as forecasted, but a full-fledged snowstorm. At our home in Granby, we already had a foot of heavy snow, and some of the upper elevations in Rocky Mountain National Park have gotten almost two feet. Just like that, the hunt for Dan Minuex was over as the National Guard and FBI tried to get over Berthoud Pass before it closed. It looked like a fast-moving parade of government and military vehicles east bound out of Grand County as they raced the storm toward Berthoud Pass and Interstate 70.

As I looked out my living room window northwest toward Rocky Mountain National Park in the far distance, all I could see was large snowflakes drifting lazily on the breeze as they fell from the cold and lonely sky and wondering if Dan Minuex was hunkered down out of the storm. Maybe he had already fled back to Kansas; maybe he was dead as the FBI experts predicted. Maybe this and maybe that; a lot of maybes with no answers. It left an uneasy feeling in the pit of my stomach. One thing that I knew for certain - I would not sleep or rest soundly until I knew that the final remaining member of the Insurgence was behind bars or dead…preferably dead.

WHEN THE SONG VANISHES

Nickey had already gone to the office. I felt guilty about that since I was still in recovery from my wound and the doctor had yet to sign off on my return to duty. Physically I was close, but mentally my mind was focused on one thing, and only one thing, and that was Dan Minuex.

Took me about an hour of thumbing through all my topographical maps to find the ones I needed. I located the most current three maps that covered the entire area of North Supply Trailhead and Edwards Sluice. Digging a little further into my collection, I was able to find the same three maps, but from twenty years prior. Not sure the older maps would help me, but I rolled them up with the newer maps and headed to the dining room table.

Walking through the living room, I turned on the stereo, and the voice of Merle Haggard swam out of the speakers with one of his new songs, "The Roots of My Raising."

The roots of my raising run deep,
I come back for the strength that I need.

After turning on the light in the dining room, I removed the centerpiece from the table and spread out the most recent topo maps. Settling into the wooden chair, I began to look at every nook and cranny of each contour, symbol, road, and trail on the maps. The closer the contours were showed the raise in elevation of every mountain on the map. The further away the contours signified a decline in elevation. All depressions on the map that indicated a gully or a wash had been labeled by the mapmakers. Each building, shelter, cabin, barn, or any structure big or small had been labeled. My gut feeling was telling me that the Insurgence members had bivouacked and had been hiding in plain sight, waiting for their chance to kidnap Laney McKay. It was some place where a lone man could still hide to outlast a search for him by over 1000 men. I just had to find it. They had called the official search for Dan Minuex off, and it now fell upon the Grand County

Sheriff's Department to continue or not to continue the search. Of course, the department had no funding for such a manhunt, so it would fall squarely on my shoulders. That was okay with me; it seemed that was how it should be.

After three hours, my eyes were tiring of following each contour line on all the newer maps. I found nothing that could have hidden one man, let alone six men. The frustration of not knowing was eating at me. Setting the newer maps aside, I grabbed the older set and just like the first set, I spent another three hours looking for any telltale sign that would jump out at me showing me what I hoped to find. Nothing clicked; no matter how hard I concentrated on the maps, I saw nothing. It was as if Dan Minuex just ceased to exist.

Rolling up the maps, I set them aside, turned off the stereo, and turned on the television to Channel 7 news. John Lindsey, the anchor for Channel 7, appeared on the tube. He was dressed in a fur-lined parka and was standing at the summit of Berthoud Pass as the snow continued to fall. I caught just the tail end of the broadcast. "A Rocky Mountain fall snowstorm has spoken and the manhunt for the fugitive and final Insurgence radical Dan Minuex has ended. It was roughly one year ago that a similar manhunt in Grand County for the serial killer Samael Amos was also called off because of severe weather. In some ways, both incidents are eerily similar; both involved the death of Grand County law enforcement personnel, and both ended with more questions than answers. Both men had fled to Rocky Mountain National Park. Samael Amos' remains were found. Will the authorities also find the remains of Dan Minuex somewhere in the remote reaches of the park? Amos' death and how he died are still shrouded in mystery. Will the same story be told of Dan Minuex? Only time will tell. This is John Lindsey, Channel 7 News."

Turning off the television, I looked out the front window again as the snow was still falling. John Lindsey and the rest of the world did know that Amos was dead, but not how he died. I was the only one that knew the entire story. If I had my way, Minuex would also be dead. Nickey, Laney, Isabella, and I needed that assurance we were safe from harm from any vengeance from a man like Minuex. I would take a bullet and gladly give up my life to keep the others safe. That was the Ute Indian warrior in me that needed to protect those whom I loved and cared for to keep them safe. Anger flooded my mind, and I swore an oath to myself that no matter what happens to me personally, I would do everything within my power to bring Minuex to justice or to kill him.

I was so lost in thought that the phone rang several times before I realized it was ringing. Walking over to the wall phone, I picked it up and said, "Hello."

"Hey dipshit, you owe me a Budweiser."

Laughing, I quickly replied, "If I remember correctly, it was a Coors Light. You sound good, Tom; you must be on the mend."

Sheriff Tom Walker chuckled, "I told that SWAT commander to shoot you if you mentioned Coors Light; luckily for you he is not there in the room with you, or you would be pushing up daisies. You know those guys are just looking for any reason to shoot someone. Seriously, Dane, it is good to hear your voice. The doctor down here in Denver said I was either the toughest or the dumbest son of a bitch he has ever had the pleasure of saving their life. I like to think even at my age I am the toughest, but you and I both know differently. Both ways, they are releasing me in a couple of days, and as soon as the storm passes, I am coming home."

"That is splendid news, Tom, and we miss you here. Did you hear the FBI has discontinued the search for Dan Minuex?"

"I just saw it on the news. That is the reason I am calling you. Truthfully Dane, I am worried about you. Having known your grandpa, dad, and having known you your entire life, I cannot help but be concerned. I don't even pretend to understand the Ute Indian connection you have with nature and that sixth sense you seem to have. What I know is when you are personally connected to a case such as this one with Minuex and the Insurgence, you have a focus like no other. You never talk about it, but I know you have premonitions, and you see things that no one else can see. Case in point is what happened after Samael Amos disappeared. I don't want you riding off into the sunset to right a wrong and get yourself into a mess of trouble you can't get out of. I want you…no, I need you to promise me that if you get a clue, a premonition, or vision that you talk to me first. Can you do that?"

The respect I had for Sheriff Tom Walker had no boundaries. I loved him like a father, and I understood his concern. But there were certain warrior attributes and honor that were ingrained into me from my Ute Indian culture that prevented me from talking to those that did not have my heritage. Tom would try to comprehend all that I told him, but his understanding would be limited and his sense of duty to the law that he was sworn to uphold would also hamper him. Clearing my voice, "Tom, you know after my father, you are the most important man in my life. You have been more than generous with your time and love for me. You gave me a job when others would not. I owe you more than I can ever repay you, but I can't promise I will talk to you first. All I can promise is that I will think about it."

There was silence on the other end of the line for what seemed a full minute before Tom spoke again, "Fair enough, Dane, fair enough."

CHAPTER 22

Nickey didn't get home until after the sun had finished its arc for the day and had disappeared behind the snow-capped mountains on the western horizon. Her face broke into a smile as she walked into the kitchen when she smelled the aroma of breaded pork chops and baked potatoes. Breaded pork chops were about the only thing I could make that was any good, and once in a great while I would make them for us. So, on this chilly autumn evening, I made dinner. Nickey drifted in behind me as I was setting the dinner plates on the table and wrapped her arms around my chest and hugged me as if there was no tomorrow. "Looks like my cowboy is just about all healed up. Thank you for making dinner, Dane." After dinner, we cuddled up on the couch and watched a movie on the television. It was a John Wayne classic western Cahill U.S. Marshal. I had not seen it before and toward the end of the movie Wayne as J. D. Cahill says, *"Well, there's no use prodding around. I'm willing to die trying to keep 'em. The question is, are you willing to die trying to take 'em. Now I'm cold and hungry and wet and tired and short-tempered, so get on with it!"* That quote rolled around in my brain pan long after the movie was over and Nickey and I were getting ready for bed. It seemed to sum up my feelings toward Dan Minuex. Whatever fate had in store for the two of us, I wished it would just get on with it!

Nickey, after brushing her teeth and seductively brushing out her hair, then stripped down to her red lace panties and a form fitting half t-shirt. This was her seduction outfit that she would wear to entice me. It worked every time.

Waking up several hours after *Mi Vida* and I had made love, the dream I just had of grandfather was the same dream as before. Squinting my eyes, I recalled his last words to me once again, *"Heed my words Dane, the one that got away is not done with you or the ones you love."*

Grandfather's words ran through my mind time and time again as I rolled onto my side facing Nickey. The window drapes were open, and the love of my life was blanketed in the half light of the moon shining through our bedroom window. Reaching out, I gently touched her hair and felt the silkiness of it as I rolled a few strands in between my forefinger and thumb. There was nothing I could think of that was better than loving this woman. Even in her sleep, she would touch the scar on her face that Amos had inflicted. Each time she did it pained me knowing I was not there to protect her from such evil. Feeling guilty at not being able to protect her then, I swore an oath to protect her now from the likes of Minuex. Focusing my mind, I brought up the image of the man the last moment I saw him before he fled at the Edwards' cabin. The words came easily, and I said them silently to myself and to that picture of Dan Minuex in my mind, "It is my nature to be kind, gentle, and loving. But know this, when it comes to matters of protecting Nickey, my friends, and my heart, do not trifle with me, for I will call upon my warrior spirit and will become the most powerful and relentless creature you have ever known! I will not let my wife be hurt again!"

Words, anger, and oaths were useless unless I knew where the man was. Rolling onto my back, I stared at the ceiling and asked silently, "Where are you, Dan Minuex?" For now, I was at his mercy and waiting for him to show himself.

Closing my eyes, I concentrated on slowing my heartbeat and in a few minutes, I welcomed the sleep as it rolled over me.

*

The next two weeks were a whirlwind of activity. Feeling good and with the doctor's blessing, I returned to work, as did the sheriff. In Tom's case, he was given light duty and was prohibited from doing field work for now. Given that restriction, of course, I teased my boss about how he had been on light duty for years prior to him being wounded. The first time I teased him with that joke, I was standing in his office, and he threw a stapler at me, knocking a hole in the drywall. The stapler was still stuck in the wall. When Tom was in the bathroom, I had taken a 5 x 8 photo of Nickey and me that had been on my desk and had taken the photo out of the frame. Then I promptly glued the frame around the hole and the stapler. Upon his return from the restroom, Tom laughed so hard he had tears in his eyes. Anyone who showed up at our office after that, Tom always took them in to show his and my handiwork.

*

Deputies John Combs, Zach Lewis, and Barry Mason were all buried on the same day during one service at the Grand Lake Cemetery. It was the same cemetery where Gene Sanford was buried; he was the deputy that Amos had killed at the same time Nickey had been attacked.

The funeral for our friends and coworkers was a lengthy somber affair with family of all giving eulogies of the three brave souls who had lost their lives in the line of duty. The burial and service were big news, and the world-wide media had once again returned to Grand County to cover the event. Thankfully, they were respectful and kept their distance.

Laney McKay and Isabella had come out of seclusion and attended the funeral. This time when Laney returned to Grand County, she had a small entourage with her. She had hired a security firm and brought with her an armed security detail of six no-nonsense bodyguards. During the service Laney sang several soul-wrenching renditions of the gospel's traditional songs such as "Amazing Grace" and "Rock of Ages." There was not a dry eye when she sang. Her voice once again, given to such classics, was just about the most beautiful thing I had ever heard.

The song that swept everyone away was Laney sang a song that had been written for the soundtrack of the 1973 film "Pat Garrett and Billy the Kid." It was an original song made popular by Bob Dylan, "Knockin' on Heaven's Door."

Mama, take this badge off of me,
I can't use it anymore
It's gettin' dark, too dark to see,
I feel like I'm knockin' on heaven's door

Rod Edwards' funeral was three days after the media had abandoned Grand County and six days after the Grand County Deputies' funeral at the same cemetery just north of Grand Lake and a stone's throw away from the burnt out Edwards Cabin just above the Edwards Sluice. The only ones in attendance at Rod's funeral were the Chaplin from Isabella's church, Laney, Nickey, myself, and three elders of the Cheyenne Tribal Council. After the Christian part of the ceremony, the Cheyenne elders who were dressed in their buckskins and headdresses of their ancestors did the Sun Dance to celebrate and honor Rod's life and death as a Dog Soldier Warrior of the Cheyenne Nation.

As they lowered Rod's casket into the ground, Laney with no music to accompany her sang the love song made popular by Leo Sayer "When I Need You."

When I need you,
I just close my eyes and I'm with you
And all that I so wanna give you,

WHEN THE SONG VANISHES

it's only a heartbeat away

We had a quiet dinner at Nickey's and my house for all those that had attended Rod's funeral, including the security detail After dessert Laney, Isabella, and their security team prepared to head back east. As I hugged Laney and Isabella just before they got into the limo that would take them to Denver and the airport, I got a sudden nervous chill up my spine. It felt like a bad omen. As the black limo pulled out on to the highway and headed toward Berthoud Pass, I watched it fade into the distance. Nickey, who had been standing by my side and holding my hand as we watched our friends drive away, looked at me, and asked, "Dane, are you okay?"

A feeling of trepidation washed over me as I turned to my wife and responded, "I just get this weird feeling that we will never see them again."

Nickey smiled and said, "Well, I for sure wouldn't blame them if they never came back to Grand County with all that had happened to them. If they don't, we can still call them on the phone and write them letters and of course listen to Laney's songs on the radio. I am sure we will see Laney from time to time on the television and on the Grammy Awards show."

"Of course, you are right *Mi Vida*, and I am just being sentimental."

"My Indian Cowboy is such a big marshmallow sometimes."

"Don't tell anyone my love because they just might yank my man card."

Nickey smiled, "Oh baby, it would take more than a little sentiment to revoke your man card. You are the manliest man I have ever known, and I love every inch of you."

Nickey Lynn stood on her tiptoes as I bent down to kiss her full on the lips. Nickey's smile got even bigger as she said, "Matter of fact mister, I am going to shower and put on the red lace panties you like so much for a little alone time."

She turned and headed into the house, leaving me alone looking toward the southwest. Of course, Nickey misunderstood my meaning when I told her about my feeling of never seeing Laney and Isabella ever again. Closing my eyes, I said a silent prayer for Laney and Isabella's safety. When I opened my eyes, I felt the wind pick up and the temperature drop suddenly, and I couldn't shake the feeling of dread that I felt.

CHAPTER 23

For the next month after the funerals, the deaths of the Grand County Sheriff deputies and Rod Edwards had a sobering and quieting effect on all of Grand County. Petty crime, drunk driving, spousal abuse, and other crimes almost came to a standstill as the residents came to terms with all that had happened. It was as if someone had pulled a large blanket over the entire county to snuff out all the cruel and ill-advised things that humans do to each other or to themselves.

The following Saturday Nickey and I both had it off and as we ate our breakfast, Nickey pointed at the topographical maps I had rolled up and stuck between the fridge and the wall and said, "I assume you had little luck looking at the topo maps of the area near North Supply Trailhead?"

"Zero luck, spent about six hours going over all the maps and saw nothing at all that could give me any sign that one man could hide from over 1000 men looking for him. It turned out to be a waste of time."

Nickey cleared off the dining room table of the breakfast dishes. Once she had completed that task, she got the topo maps and spread them out onto the table. "I am going to take a look see. Curious what it all looks like on a map; I want to follow our path that we took that night from the trailhead to Edwards Sluice while it is still somewhat fresh in my memory."

The newer maps were on top of the older ones, and I spent about an hour showing Nickey the path we took that night. Looking at the maps, we relived the battle and escape from our campsite near North Supply Creek to Isabella's cabin, and it brought more than a few tears to our eyes remembering the ones we lost along the way. As Nickey rolled up the newer maps and started looking at the older maps, I went to get dressed. We had decided to spend the day riding our horses - Nickey's gelding Cochise and my new mare Ranger. Just as I stomped on my last cowboy boot, Nickey yelled out from the kitchen to me, "Dane, what's this symbol? It is not on the newer maps."

That got my attention. Hurrying into the kitchen as I buckled my belt, I said, "Show me what you are looking at."

Nickey pointed to a small black rectangle not more than a quarter of a mile from the trailhead of North Supply Creek. It was a small rectangle, and it was in between two contour lines. The contour lines were so close together to the rectangle it was difficult to tell it was there. So much in fact, I had missed it during the time I spent studying the map. Grabbing a pencil from the junk drawer, I drew a circle around it and then grabbed the newer map that was the same as the one with the rectangle Nickey had pointed out. Flipping back and forth, I realized the rectangle was not on the newer map. Thinking to myself, but saying it out loud, "I will be damned, it is not on the newer map."

Nickey looked and sounded confused, "Not following. What is that symbol? Is it important?"
Double checking once again that it was not present on the newer map, I turned to Nickey and then pointed to the symbol on the older map. "That symbol represents a structure, probably a small cabin. Notice how it is almost touching the contour lines on both

sides. That means someone built the structure or cabin at the bottom of a gully."

Nickey's face still showed confusion when she said, "Seems sort of unwise to me to build a cabin in a gully. Wouldn't that create all kinds of problems with snow drifting and make it more difficult to get too?"

I looked more closely now at the contours leading up to and away from the structure. "As for the snow, you wouldn't care if the cabin was only seasonal. As for it being difficult to get to, that was the whole idea. I believe what you found and what I missed is an old moonshiner's cabin where they probably had a copper still to make whiskey. They would have wanted it hidden from prying eyes, not just from the law, but also from rival moonshiners. Follow my finger on the map. The cabin is located in a very narrow gully that is closed in on both sides. You could literally walk within twenty-five yards of it on both sides and never see it. A perfect hideaway for a moonshiner…or six men waiting for the right time to kidnap Laney."

Nickey's face showed understanding as a smile crept across her face as she said, "Or a lone man waiting out a search party of over 1000 men."

"Exactly! It might mean nothing, and just like the new map shows, it might not even be there at all. We were going to ride the horses today. What do you think of loading them up in the trailer and taking them to the North Supply Creek trailhead and looking for the cabin?"

Nickey was excited and said, "Sounds as if we have a mission. Let's do it."

Nickey and I spoke little as we drove to where we boarded the horses just a couple of miles north of Granby. We used to make this trip every day to feed the horses, but with time constraints from work, it made that almost impossible, so we ended up hiring the couple that we boarded from to feed our horses daily.

Both Cochise and Ranger were excited to see us, and they started snorting and pawing the ground with their hooves in anticipation of getting out of the corral to be ridden. Cochise was the horse that saved my life in my confrontation with Amos almost a year ago. The gelding did not belong to me. He was Nickey's horse, but he would never be sold and would live out his days here in Grand County. I owed him everything. Cochise, who was Nickey's four year old gelding Appaloosa, was the first out of the barn and pacing the corral fence in anticipation of some time with Nickey. Cochise's chest and front legs were ebony black, and his hindquarters looked as if someone had spilled twenty gallons of white paint, which gave him the most beautiful mixture of black and snow I had ever seen on a horse. He was gentle and about fifteen hands high and was the perfect size for Nickey. Cochise barely tolerated me but loved Nickey Lynn like no other. Ranger, my mare breed, was a Colorado Ranger. She was seventeen hands tall, very athletic, had endurance, and was dark brown and spotted like a leopard with white spots on her hindquarters. I had bought Ranger several months ago replacing my mare Thunder who had been killed by Amos last year when I tracked him down in Rocky Mountain National Park. The Colorado Ranger breed is descended from two stallions imported from Turkey to the US state of Virginia in the late 1800's. They then bred these stallions to be ranch horses in Nebraska and Colorado, and in the early 1900's the two stallions who every registered Colorado Ranger traced to Patches #1 and Max #2, were foaled. Rancher Mike Ruby, who founded the Colorado Ranger Horse Association in 1935, championed the breed.

After hooking up to our horse trailer that we kept at the same place we boarded Cochise and Ranger, the horses were eager to load after we saddled them. We pulled on to HWY 34 heading north at nine a.m., heading toward Rocky Mountain National Park and the trailhead at North Supply Creek.

WHEN THE SONG VANISHES

Nickey plugged in the cassette by Billy Crash Craddock. They called the album Crash, and the first song on it was named "Broken Down in Tiny Pieces." Both Nickey and I sang along with the song as it played.

Take me back to where I started,
You can help me mend
Here I am in tiny pieces,
Please put me back together again

In less than forty-five minutes, we pulled off the plowed county road into the unplowed parking lot at the North Creek Trailhead. Getting out of the Chevy Blazer, we could feel the nippy air on this late autumn day at this elevation. The sun was riding a blue sky with no clouds, and it felt good on my face. It had not snowed since the snowstorm that had ended the manhunt for Dan Minuex, but the temperatures had stayed low enough that it had hardly melted and there was still a good twelve to fourteen inches of snow on the ground.

There were only two sets of vehicle tracks in the parking lot - ours and another set that was several weeks old. The sun and the wind had worn the older set down to the point you could no longer see the tread of the tires, but they were there, nonetheless.

As we unloaded Cochise and Ranger, I noticed a set of footprints in the snow headed north, the same direction we would be heading. Crouching down, I studied the footprints. And they were also several weeks old and had been worn down by the elements.

Standing up, I walked a short distance to a tree and found one print in the shadows that was not as deteriorated. Nickey watched me as I studied the tracks. "Sort of strange there is only one set of tracks."
The track in the shadows had been preserved well enough that I could see a partial print of the boot that made it. Standing up, I looked north and then looked back south toward the parking lot

and Nickey. "Whoever made this boot print, Nickey, was not heading into the woods; the tracks are heading out of the woods. Since the last snowstorm, it was a one-way trip, meaning they were already in the forest before the big snow. After the storm they walked out here and probably caught a ride in whatever vehicle left those other tire tracks in the parking lot."

"Do you think it was Minuex?"

The one-way tracks were a mystery. Still studying the boot tracks, I said, "Might mean nothing, but it is possible. We are going to follow the tracks and look for that cabin. I need to know if it was Minuex. I have to know how he eluded the manhunt and disappeared."

CHAPTER 24

Nickey and I decided that taking our service pistols, - my 357 3-screw Ruger Blackhawk, and Nickey's Ruger Security-Six double-action revolver chambered for a 38 round - would be prudent. We had also decided we should take both of our Ruger M-14 rifles for good measure. We did not know what lay ahead on the trail, so it was best to be prepared.

After belting on our service holsters, I slid my rifle into the scabbard on the side of Ranger. Looking at Nickey, "We need to treat this just like we have a suspect still in the woods and exercise every caution. I will take point and you bring up the rear guard. We will refrain from talking and use hand signals as we follow the boot tracks."

Taking out of my vest pocket the now folded older topo map, I got a bearing with my compass, and our path was in the same directions as the tracks that had come from the woods. Stepping into my stirrup, I planted my butt into the saddle and Nickey did likewise. It felt good to be on a horse again, and it was times like these that I envied my ancestors that lived their entire lives on the backs of horses. Moving out slowly, we headed north, following the boot tracks.

Stopping only once to get another compass bearing, and since our destination was not far, we made the steep incline of the gully in about an hour. The boot tracks that had ended up in the parking lot were in fact a straight beeline to the gully on the map. We could see our breath in the chilled mountain air as we dismounted. Tying Cochise and Ranger off to an evergreen tree branch, I pointed to the north, then spoke in a whisper, "According to the map, the hidden gully begins at that top of that rise."

Nickey nodded her head "yes" acknowledging my statement. Pulling the Ruger M-14 from my scabbard, I used the rifle sling and swung it over my back. After taking my field binoculars from my saddlebag, Nickey and I climbed the incline toward the top of the ridge line.

Reaching the top of the ridge, we inched our way over the top and just like the older map showed, there was a small cabin at the bottom of the gully. Using my binoculars, I scanned the cabin and the entire gully. The boot tracks we had followed went over the ridge and straight to the cabin. It was even more obvious now that whoever had walked out after the snowstorm had been in that cabin. By the looks of the construction of the cabin, it was ancient, probably fifty or sixty years old. I knew what we were looking at were the remains of an old moonshiner's cabin. The gully was short and narrow and at the top was only thirty yards across; it was the perfect place to build a hideout. If the search party was using the more modern topo maps, they would never have known about this cabin unless they accidentally came upon it. The reason they had never seen it from the air is that it was tucked in under some enormous evergreen trees. Even now, as I was looking at it, it was nearly invisible to the naked eye. Being cautious, we watched the cabin for a full thirty minutes for any sign of life.

Feeling confident that the cabin and the hidden gully were void of any human life, Nickey and I moved slowly down into the gully with our service revolvers drawn just in case.

WHEN THE SONG VANISHES

The cabin door was not locked, and it barely stayed on its hinges as I gradually pushed it open. Stepping into the cabin, I could smell the stink of decaying wood as I surveyed the interior. The cabin was a one-room affair with a fireplace and one rough-hewed table with four matching chairs. Holstering my pistol since the cabin was empty except for the furniture and some backpacks stacked in the corner, I stepped back out of the door and said to Nickey, "Come on in, there is nobody home."

Nickey and I made sure we were wearing gloves as we quickly searched the cabin. The backpacks when counted totaled six. There were six sleeping bags, camp stoves, utensils, and various clothing such as flannel shirts, socks, and jeans. We also found freeze-dried food to sustain six men for another month or one man for six months. There was no doubt in my mind we were standing in the hideout that the Insurgence used after the bank robbery in Grand Lake and were waiting until the opportune time to kidnap Laney McKay. This was also the same place that when the kidnaping went awry that Dan Minuex returned to so he could hide and wait out the manhunt that had been mounted looking for his capture. This old moonshiner's cabin was now a crime scene.

One of the odd things I found in the cabin was a wooden crate, and when I slowly opened it, I found it full of comic books and magazines. The comic book on top was an issue of Archie with a cartoon of Archie, Betty, Reggie, Jughead and Veronica on the cover. Picking it up by the corner, I turned to Nickey, "Can you imagine six battle hardened Vietnam veterans turned radical Insurgence members reading the adventures of Archie, Jughead and the rest of their crew?"

Nickey laughed and replied, "Never underestimate the power of a good comic book."

"I always thought Veronica was hot, but not as hot as my wife."

That brought more laughter from Nickey, "Good save there, mister."

I laid the Archie comic book back on top of the others in the wooden crate and wondered if the Insurgence radicals brought the comic books to read to help pass the time or if they were already stashed here by the previous occupant. Probably one clue among many to this case I would never know.

Nickey and I searched the cabin like police investigators, always being careful what we touched, knowing that once we got back home and called the FBI, they would send their own forensics' team here to thoroughly go through the cabin and everything in it. Once we were done in the cabin, Nickey and I sat on the front porch for a spell looking at the lay of the land. It was not surprising that no one stumbled upon this cabin during the manhunt. The gully was small like a knife slice in the earth with steep sides. The topo maps the search party would have been using would not have showed the cabin in this gully, and it was not visible from the air. How Minuex and his crew knew of its existence, I will never know, but they knew and used it cunningly.

Since sitting on the porch, I had done some deep thinking and had said nothing until finally Nickey asked, "What's bothering you?"

I looked her in the eyes, and she obviously saw and felt my concern. How could I ever explain the remorse I was feeling at this very moment? How could she ever know the responsibility I felt that four good men died that night when confronted by Dan Minuex and the others by my reacting to the events as they unfolded? I should have been acting and taking command and made the Insurgence members react to me. I had been in charge; it was my obligation to see that those men made it home alive that night to their loved ones. The guilt of failing in that regard was eating me alive. It seemed I had failed at every avenue that night and now. Even this cabin was a failure; I missed it on the map. Nickey's face now showed concern when I tried to answer her question, "Just feeling a little down right now. That will change. That I promise you. I have some guilt over what happened that night when Rod and the others had been killed. I feel I didn't do enough to bring them all home. Also feeling stupid that I didn't see the cabin on the older topo maps. If I had when I first looked at them, Dan Minuex was probably still here in the cabin, still in Grand County. We might have ended this right here."

Nickey put her arms around me and hugged me tight. "You are a good man, Dane Lee. You are not to blame for what happened that night. Matter of fact, it was your actions that saved Isabella, Laney, Tom, and me. The blame rides squarely on the shoulders of all those Insurgence members, alive or dead, and no one else. It is going to be dark soon, and we better head out and call the FBI. I am sure they will have agents up here in the morning; therefore, we need to be well rested when they get here."

Nickey then tilted her head, and we kissed a long kiss. It felt good to have such a woman by my side. Standing up, I looked back toward the front door of the cabin and said, "One thing we now know for sure is that Dan Minuex hid out here in this cabin during the manhunt. What we do not know at this moment is where he is now, and what he plans to do about the death of his Insurgence members, especially his brother Mitch."

CHAPTER 25

Nickey was right about Ken Ekross and his team of investigators from the FBI showing up first thing on Sunday morning. Having to show the FBI where the old moonshiner's cabin was, that ended up being the hideout for the Insurgence, gave Nickey and me another day with Cochise and Ranger. The FBI investigators hiked in behind us. Ekross was the first into the cabin and spent maybe thirty minutes in there by himself before he turned it over to his team. Having done that, he admired considerably Cochise and Ranger. Ranger was loving it when the G-man was nuzzling his hand up and down her neck. Ken was all smiles as he was doing so. Looking at me and with that big grin of his, he said, "I envy both Nickey and yourself. You work in law enforcement, but you live in what is probably the most beautiful part of the state. Hell, maybe in the entire country."

Nodding my head in affirmation, "I have lived here my entire life. My ancestors once called these mountains for 500 square miles their home. You envy us; I envied them. They fought and died for their beliefs, but they were free of all the rules and laws of civilization. Their lives were simpler, but they were free. Freer than you or I will ever be."

Ken was running what I said through his mind as he was enjoying his time with the horses when I asked him, "Do you have any leads on the whereabouts of Dan Minuex?"

"We have more than we can count since every Laney McKay and country music fan is on the lookout for him, but, none of the tips to his whereabouts have turned out to be any good. The manpower and money spent on chasing these leads is unbelievable. Maybe, he left behind a clue or two here in the cabin, but I doubt it. Dan Minuex just disappeared. Maybe he is dead, like some believe, I just don't know. The higher-ups in the department are ready to pull the plug on any continuing investigation since we are hemorrhaging money on this case. I suspect within a week they will shut down any active investigation and move on to newer and more urgent cases that have popped up."

Ken and his FBI team left Grand County on Tuesday and they took everything - backpacks, table, chairs, and even the wooden crate with the comic books back to Denver. Each item was evidence and was packaged and sealed for the trip back to the Denver FBI office.

*

After the FBI visit to the remote moonshiner's cabin, the autumn and winter months flew by with no word on the whereabouts of Dan Minuex. The FBI had, as Ken Ekross had stated with no leads, closed their ongoing investigation one week after their last visit to Grand County. I almost believed that Dan Minuex had died as some believed…almost. My gut was telling me he was alive and being careful, cautious, and waiting until no one was looking for him anymore. My gut was telling me he was one of the most dangerous predators. Although he had not shown himself, it felt as if he was just biding his time to exact his revenge on those that had a hand in the killing of his team members and brother.

Grandfather Matt Lee had been silent and had not made an appearance in my dreams until the dark of Sunday morning on May 22nd. This one was different. I woke up at three a.m. bathed in sweat. Closing my eyes, I tried to recall the dream. *The dream had come in two waves - the first part was grandfather and I were standing on a corner of a busy street in a city. Not in Colorado and not in the mountains, which confused me, for I never dreamed of grandfather away from the mountains. As we looked in the distance, there were hundreds of people gathered as if they were waiting for something or someone. The crowd was in good spirits and joyful. I looked at grandfather for some sort of explanation and he just nodded toward the crowd in the distance as if I should focus my attention there. So, I did. Just as I turned my attention back to the crowd, gunshots rang out from somewhere in the distance. The joyful multitude of people now turned into a panic as they all scrambled to move away from the center of the crowd. People were tripping and falling as they fled. As soon as the gunfire began, my dream slowed down as if everything was in slow motion. So slow that I could count each gunshot, and they totaled eight, one right after another. The sequence of the shots told me even in my dream state that there was only one shooter. My sense of what was happening told me the shooter was not in the crowd as first believed, but they had shot into the gathering. Who or what the target was I did not know, and grandfather was not forthcoming in any explanation. Feeling anxious, confused, and nervous about the event unfolding before my eyes, my feeling was grandfather was showing me of something that was to be. Maybe an event in the future. The first wave of the dream faded to black, and the next wave came out of the darkness, became focused and clear, and now grandfather and I were standing in a meadow next to a small creek. I could feel the wind on my face, and I could hear the trickle of the water flowing in the creek. Once again, we were not in the Rocky Mountains, but some place where the landscape was flat and there was not one tree to be seen. Still confused, I once again looked to grandfather for some understanding of what was to be and where we were, and he pointed behind me. I turned sluggishly with a sense of trepidation. He was pointing at an old house in the distance that was at the end of a white rock road. The two-story house was built like the old Victorian houses I had seen in the old mining towns, but this house was not in the mountains. This Victorian house was in the country, but in a place that I had never been before. The house was painted in a light brown color that reminded me of sand. The roof shingles were red, and the roof extended into an overhang that covered a large front porch. As I looked at the house in the distance, I wondered what the connection was to me and if it was connected to the first part of my dream. Looking to grandfather for an explanation, I received none other than he repeated his words once again from my previous dreams, "The one of French descent will hide, wait, and strike when you least expect it. My words to you, my grandson, are to take the battle to him where he least expects it. Take the war to where he lays his head at night."*

Slowly sitting up in bed as to not disturb Nickey, I kept running the dream through my mind searching for clues that could help me find Minuex. Not sure how I knew it, but I thought that the first part of the dream in the city was in the future. How far into the future I did not have a clue. There had been a crowd and eight gunshots. Who was doing the shooting? Who were they shooting at? The second part of the dream about the old Victorian house, I had no feeling one way or the other if it was now or in the future. Maybe it was both. One thing I knew was that both dreams centered on Dan Minuex.

The bedside clock was now flashing 4:00 a.m. Knowing there was no way in hell that I would fall back to sleep now, I decided to get up and make some breakfast for Nickey and me.

No blueberry pop tarts and Tang this morning; I decided on ham and cheese omelets smothered in Nickey's leftover green chili made with roasted chilies. Green chili was its own food group here in Colorado and was a staple of all folks from Colorado. Nickey had never seen, nor heard of, nor tasted green chili before moving to Colorado. Now she had mastered the art of preparing it, and her green chili was some of the best I had ever eaten.

The smell of the omelets had wakened Nickey, and she walked into the kitchen to get her morning cup of coffee in a half shirt and a black pair of lace panties. Her hair had yet to be brushed and still had that bedroom look. I promptly burnt my finger on the burner as I turned to watch her walk by.

Moving quickly to the kitchen sink to run cold water over my fast-turning red pointy finger, Nickey looked seductively over her shoulder back at me, "Were you staring at my butt."

"I was, and it might turn into an emergency room hospital visit after being distracted and burning my finger."

Laughing, Nickey said, "That will teach you, mister. Hoping my cowboy will fully recover."

Now it was my turn to laugh, "The burnt finger? That would be a yes. From looking at your booty? That would be a no. That awesome derriere will get me into trouble from time to time."

Nickey finally got her coffee and sat down as I sat her omelet in front of her. After turning on the television to the news in the living room, I sat down with my breakfast.

Nickey and I had just started to eat our breakfast when John Lindsey, the anchor for Channel 7 news, appeared on the tube, "AP Bulletin is now reporting that the shooting in downtown Nashville, Tennessee last night during a fan autograph session outside the famous recording studio RCA Studio A has claimed the lives of five. It is official that America's country sweetheart Laney McKay is dead!"

CHAPTER 26

Nickey and I just stared in numb silence at the television as John Lindsey gave more details, "Country music's latest and greatest Laney McKay was just finishing up the final recording session of her new album "Take Me Home" and had been scheduled to sign autographs for one hour on the sidewalk that was just outside of the studio. It was a much-anticipated event since no one had seen McKay in public since the failed kidnapping that ended up with nine dead in her home state of Colorado. Along with McKay, those dead on the streets of Nashville were Laney's constant companion Isabella Edwards and three members of her security detail - Donzell Verdun, Carlo Cavazutti, and Kurt Kling. It seems the eight shots came from the roof of a five story building across the street. Police descended on the building and quickly made their way to the rooftop, but apparently the shooter had already fled the scene."

The dream in the city with grandfather had not been of a future event. It had already happened. I had seen the dream of the death of our friends after the fact. I just didn't know it had already happened. The sense of overwhelming guilt at not being able to save Laney, Isabella, and the others flooded over me. If I had only

made better decisions on that night that we had fought the
Insurgence or that I had seen the structure of the moonshiner's
cabin the first time I looked at the topo maps. I should have been
able to prevent all this death. Nickey's tears filled her eyes as she
stared at the television as Channel 7 news did a memorial of
Laney's songs and photos. The last song they played was her
biggest hit, "Long Days, Lonely Nights."

Can't count the miles,
Or the months of emptiness
Shed a million tears,
I recall the sound of your voice

After the memorial, Nickey looked at me as the tears rolled down
her face and in a shaky voice said, "Do you think it was him?"

That is when my tears welled up in my eyes as I nodded my head,
"Yes, grandfather showed me in a dream last night. We were
standing on a street in a city looking at a crowd when the shots
were fired. I didn't see anyone get hit, just the crowd scrambling
for cover with no idea who the target was. I thought he was
showing me something that had not happened yet. This morning I
had been replaying it through my mind, trying to puzzle out what it
all meant. I did not know it had already happened. It is my fault
Nickey. I should have been better that night when we fought them
at the campground and Edwards' cabin. I should have seen the
moonshiner's cabin on the old topo map before you did. This is my
fault, and I own this."

Nickey stood and walked over to me and rolled into my arms as
she sat on my lap. Looking me straight into my soul with her red-
rimmed eyes, "I love you with all my heart and passion. None of
this is your fault, Dane, none of it. If not for you, we would have
all died that night at Edwards Sluice. The one that owns this is that
bastard Dan Minuex. The Insurgence and Minuex invaded our
sanctuary. He and the other members created this problem; they
came here to our home and engaged us. We were just living our
lives, and they brought their brand of illicit affairs to us. We didn't
ask them here; we didn't want them here; and we sure as hell

didn't want to be involved in their radical ideals. The question now is how far are we going to take it?

How are we now going to react? He killed Laney and Isabella out of revenge. Are we next?"

This woman that I had chosen to live with the rest of my life gave me strength, courage, and honor. I loved her more than anything, and at this very moment I was glad she was by my side. The guilt I was feeling faded as I realized she was right. The Insurgence radicals had invaded our sanctuary - our home - and Dan Minuex needed to know that he had awakened the killer instinct in me. Samael Amos had awakened that same predisposition just over a year-ago. The death of Amos in the cold and snow was something I was not proud of, and no one could know the truth about how he died. The death of Amos only showed what I was capable of. What I found deep within me was ugly, fierce, and deadly. An ancient warrior's spirit heightened my heartbeat and clarified my resolve. The killer instinct that I knew should be kept hidden and locked away in a civilized society. But here we are, and Minuex had brought it back to the surface. I needed to find the man. There would be no judge, jury, or a life sentence for what he had done. He needed to die, plain and simple. Looking at *Mi Vida*, I replied, "It is obvious that Minuex is not giving up until he has completed his revenge. Nickey, with no misgivings, I feel Minuex needs to die because I know given time he will come looking for us. I need to take the battle to him; I just don't know where."

*

Officially there were no suspects, or at least that the news outlets reported. Some reporters were asking the authorities, including the FBI, if the kidnapping attempt in Grand County was tied into Laney's and Isabella's deaths. If the investigating teams thought so, they were not telling. All they would say was, "This is an ongoing investigation and we cannot comment on it at this time."

Nickey and I did our due diligence in trying to stay safe right after the murders of Laney, Isabella, and the members of the security teams. Even though there were no suspects that had been named yet in their deaths, I knew in my gut it was Dan Minuex. He had plotted his revenge against the one that had killed his brother and carried it out with stealth and daring. I also knew that Nickey and I were the only ones left who had fought Minuex and his team, killing several of them in the fight at the campground and the Edwards' cabin. I knew he would come gunning for us. To the best of our abilities, we tried to change our routines and always tried to travel even to work together. I was not so worried about myself in what happens to me, but I sure as hell was worried about Nickey. Once again, I was reacting to Minuex's actions, not causing him to react to my actions. I needed to come up with a plan to change that. Laney McKay's security team members who had been killed had funerals almost immediately after their deaths in their associated home towns. There was only a small snippet in the Rocky Mountain News and Denver Post newspapers. I saw nothing on the televised networks about them.

Isabella Edwards' funeral was the Friday before Memorial Day, May 27th. Isabella was buried in the Edwards family plot next to her son and husband in the Grand Lake cemetery. There was no media present for the sendoff of such a wonderful soul. Isabella was the last of the Edwards' and there was no family left to attend the service. The only ones in attendance at Isabella's funeral were the Chaplin from the Edwards' church; Sheriff Tom Walker; three Cheyenne women that I did not know; four FBI agents who kept their distance; three elders of the Cheyenne Tribal Council; Nickey, and me. After the Christian part of the ceremony, the Cheyenne elders who were dressed in their buckskins and headdresses of their ancestors did the Sun Dance to celebrate and honor Isabella.

Isabella's death hit Nickey the hardest. That moment, and the feelings that had been shared between the two of them the morning we started looking for Rod and Laney, had connected them spiritually. Every day since Isabella's murder, Nickey went through the motions of living her life, but her sad eyes told the truth. I knew the grief that she felt was an overpowering feeling and that it would take some time for her to recover. All I could do was be there for her in the darkest moments of sorrow that she was experiencing.

For myself, the sense of guilt returned as I stood there looking down into the hole that had been dug for the casket. There were the feelings of helplessness and anger that flooded over me like an ocean wave. I needed to avenge such a wonderful woman's death. Laney McKay's funeral was the following Friday, June 3rd, after Memorial Day. Laney's family also had a family plot in the Grand Lake cemetery, and that was where Laney would be laid to rest. The three days leading up to the funeral were a freaking circus with every news outlet for the Denver area, plus many from all across the United States making their way to Grand County. Her funeral, just like her attempted kidnapping, had turned into a full-blown media event. It was disheartening to me how the news outlets had showed up and were interviewing everyone who would even look their way. Nickey and I turned down each invitation to be interviewed. It felt as if the vultures had descended. Mostly it just angered me that they showed no respect for Laney; they just wanted the newest scoop to put their name to on the AP wire. The funeral itself was a somber affair as Laney's younger sister Tracy sang "Amazing Grace" and "Rock of Ages" and Laney's signature song "Long Days, Lonely Nights." Tracy's voice was eerily identical to her older sister's voice and brought tears to almost everyone in attendance. It was a dismal day for the McKay family, Grand County, Colorado, and the rest of the country. To lose someone as beautiful in spirit as Laney saddened everyone who knew her or had seen her on the television and listened to her songs.

After they had lowered Laney's casket into the ground and the folks in attendance started to slowly drift away, special agent Ken Ekross made his way toward Nickey and myself. "Dane, do you have a moment? I would like to speak to you alone."

"Anything you might have to say to me, Ken, you can say in front of Nickey."

The government man looked at Nickey for a few seconds deciding if he would continue or not, and then his eyes shifted back to me and he spoke, "I thought I needed to inform you that none of the evidence collected at the moonshiner's cabin shows that Dan Minuex is still alive or was even there after the shoot-out at the Edwards' cabin. Those in upper management of the FBI, given the time span between the attempted kidnapping and the death of Miss McKay, do not believe that he was involved in her death. No one has heard from or has seen Minuex since you saw him do his vanishing act at the Edwards' cabin. They believe that the man is dead as some agency profilers have suggested."

Rolling my eyes to match Nickey's eye roll in disbelief, "Well, who in the hell do they think killed Laney and Isabella?"

"The same profilers are putting forth that it was a disgruntled fan of Laney's. Some kook that Laney may have not answered his love letter or did not have time to sign their autograph. Their theory is that it was some nutcase that felt slighted by Laney in some fashion, and they are focusing all their investigation and resources into that avenue for now."

Feeling the anger build within me, "If that is all true, why were there FBI agents at Isabella's funeral and here again today?"

"The only reason FBI agents and I were at both funerals is that your boss Tom Walker raised a stink when told of the direction of the Minuex case. He felt it was mandatory that we provided surveillance in case Minuex came gunning for Nickey and yourself. The Denver office did so reluctantly, but as a courtesy to Sheriff Walker - here we are. The main office back in Washington does not know we are here. As of today, there will be no more FBI surveillance or manpower in Grand County."

Knowing full well that agent Ken Ekross had no obligation to tell Nickey and me anything about the ending of the search and the investigation into Dan Minuex, I appreciated him telling us. Discouraged by the lack of effort of trying to locate Minuex, I now knew Nickey and I were on our own. Reaching out I shook the hand of the man who had become Nickey's and my friend. "I know your hands are tied in this regard, Ken, and I appreciate your letting us know."

After shaking hands, Ken looked me in the eye and reached in his coat and produced a thin manila file and handed it to me. "If you are the man I think you are and what I think you are capable of, you might want this. Just know that if anyone asks, it didn't come from me."

As Ken turned away, he said, "Keep in touch, Dane."

The ending of the conversation with special agent Ken Ekross was not only mysterious, but bizarre. Nickey even stated the obvious, "That was strange. Wonder what is in the file?"

As I opened the file so Nickey and I both could see the contents. There were no identifying logos showing this was an official FBI investigative report, but I knew better. Ken had removed all references to the FBI. It was an updated report on all probable locations and or hiding places that Dan Minuex might be. All the towns listed were in Lane County, Kansas. The town of Dighton was the only name I was familiar with since it appeared many times in the Insurgence file. The others such as Amy, Healy, Shields, and Alamota, I had never heard of. Ken had given me exactly what I needed…a starting place to look for Dan Minuex.

CHAPTER 27

After returning home from Laney's funeral, I sat down at the kitchen table and read the file that Ken had given me. The first page I had already read many months ago but reread it again. It summarized Minuex. The photo of Dan had been taken of him in what looked like a mop-up action in Vietnam. In the full body photo of Dan, he was wearing the typical tiger-striped jungle fatigues with a matching tiger-striped boonie-hat. He looked as you would expect of a soldier in combat, and that was he was fit and trim. His face was hard and lean with piercing eyes. According to his bio, he was born in Lane County, Kansas, and by all accounts his upbringing was that of a typical farm kid. His grades were in the top ten percent of his class. After graduation he joined the military and showed enough aptitude to be given a slot in the Green Berets and had risen to the rank of Master Sergeant and was a weapons specialist and served in Vietnam with the 5th Special Forces Group, who had their headquarters in Nha Trang. He served three tours in country. He was highly decorated and was honorably discharged. His age now was thirty-two years old.

The second page was a description of the history of Posse Comitatus, also known as Sheriff's Posse Comitatus. It is a loosely knit, nationwide organization established in the late 1960's and early 1970's. The group's objectives include resisting statutory authority related to federal, state, and local taxing authorities; limiting the capability of federal, state, and local law enforcement officers; and limiting access of all law enforcement representatives in trespassing on individual property. The FBI is/was conducting an extremist white hate investigation concerning the Posse Comitatus from 1972 through 1977. This extreme right-wing group takes its name from the Latin for "power of the county." Its founders, Henry Beach and William Potter Gale, were radical loyalists who claimed that the county is the highest and only legitimate level of government to which citizens owe allegiance. It is only the county, they argue, headed by a sheriff chosen by the community's white male residents that possesses the right to enforce the law. According to Posse doctrine, the law itself is derived from the Bible, English common law, the Articles of Confederation, and more vaguely, the U.S. Constitution. In their minds, no legislature or Congress has the ability to make laws that "Real Americans" are obliged to follow. Beach, a member of the pro-Nazi Silver Shirts movement during the 1930's, and Gale, a former World War II army officer and a key figure in the development of the racist and anti-Semitic Christian Identity ideology, organized the Posse Comitatus in Portland, Oregon, in 1969 in the midst of the Vietnam War and the country's racial tensions. But it was during the early to mid-1970, and in the Great Plains, that this loosely connected organization, whose members sought to keep their anonymity, achieved prominence. The farm crisis of these years created the conditions necessary for their doctrine to attract significant support. Such Posse figures as Gordon Kahl, a North Dakota farmer, James Wickstrom, the Posse's self-proclaimed "counterinsurgency director," and Rick Elliot, a Colorado dairy farmer who became the publisher of the anti-Semitic Primrose and Cattlemen's Gazette (its message being that Jews were leading cattlemen down the primrose path), crisscrossed the region explaining to farmers and ranchers why they were under no obligation to repay overdue loans or peacefully accept the foreclosure of their property. This appealed to some indebted and hard-pressed farmers whose entire way of life was in jeopardy. At "seminars" and on country music radio stations such as KTTL-FM in Dodge City, Kansas, Posse spokesmen explained to their listeners that they were under no obligation to pay income taxes to a fraudulent Internal Revenue Service or abide by the judgments of federal or state courts. According to FBI reports, in 1976, the Posse had seventy-eight chapters in twenty-three states, concentrated mostly in the Great Plains and the Midwest. Some Posse figures attempted to transform their rhetoric about resisting the government and cleansing the land into reality. Violent encounters between law enforcement officers and Posse members attracted widespread attention. Posse members threatened or carried out violent attacks on individuals they defined as their enemies. The Posse Comitatus continues to be an intermittently active faction of antigovernment protest.

The third page was a brief history of the Insurgence. Roughly one year ago (1975-1976) there was a falling out in the Posse's leadership. Six of the younger members that had recently finished their tours in Vietnam had become dissatisfied in what they thought was a non-aggressive direction that the Posse was moving. These six members are all highly trained individuals from the Special Forces with over 100 combat missions among them. One (Mitch Minuex, now deceased) was a helicopter pilot who flew in over thirty combat missions in Vietnam and Cambodia. The Insurgence goal was to overthrow the government. Since the Posse in their minds was useless in the endeavor to do so, the six split off and formed what we now know as 'The Insurgence.' To fund their overthrow, they resorted to robbing banks. They would execute each bank robbery with clockwork military planning and organization. They would steal a helicopter and then they would pick a small-town bank where law enforcement is spread thin so they expect little or no resistance. The Insurgence saw themselves as patriots. After a bank robbery and a failed kidnap of Laney McKay in Grand County, Colorado, five of the Insurgence members were killed in a running battle with the Grand County Sheriff's department. One (Dan Minuex) did escape and went missing but is now presumed dead.

WHEN THE SONG VANISHES

The fourth page was a map of Lane County, Kansas. The boundaries of the county formed almost a perfect square in western Kansas. To the west of Lane County was Scott County; to the north was Gove County; to the east was Ness County; and to the south was Finney County. The topo map of this area showed no hills or anything other than flat land with a few small creeks. Dighton was almost dead center of the county and was at the crossroads of two small highways - highway 96 which runs east and west and highway 23 which runs north to south. The smaller town or township of Amy was due west of Dighton. Healy was northwest; Shields was due north; and Alamota was southwest of Dighton. At the bottom of the map, someone had handwritten a note, "Lane County is an agriculture community. County population is 1,876, making it the third-least populous county in Kansas. County seat is Dighton, which is the only true city in the county. They named the county after James H. Lane, who was a leader of the Jayhawker abolitionist movement and served as one of the first U.S. Senators from Kansas."

The fifth page broke down the potential connections that Dan Minuex may use to hide by township or town.

Amy, Kansas - John Lynch, a wheat farmer who also raises cattle. Not a known member of the Posse Comitatus but is a close friend and high school classmate of Dan Minuex.

Healy, Kansas - Bryan Cherry, a wheat, milo, and alfalfa, farmer. A first cousin to the Minuex's and a known member of Posse Comitatus. The second name in Healy was Eric Sanders who was a close high school friend of Dan who lived in the town of Healy. Sanders was a tractor and auto mechanic there. He was not a known member of the Posse Comitatus.

Shields, Kansas - Bart & Brett Chipman, twins who operated the grain elevator in Shields. Not known members of the Posse Comitatus. Close friends of the Minuex brothers in high school. From the map and the addresses, I could not determine where their houses were exactly. They could be in town or in the country. Both had to be checked out.

Alamota, Kansas - Irvin Maddox, known member of the Posse Comitatus. Cattle rancher and wheat farmer. Ex-brother-in-law of the Minuex brothers.

Dighton, Kansas - Harvey and Rip Minuex, known members of the Posse Comitatus. Wheat, alfalfa, and milo farmers. Uncles of the Minuex brothers.

The sixth and final page of the file gave a short summary note of the surveillance of each friend and relative mentioned on page five. After quickly reading all the notes, I realized the notes said the same thing and that was Dan Minuex had not been sighted in Lane County by the FBI agents during their surveillance. It also stated that those mentioned in the reports seemed to go about their daily chores and business without interruption. The report gave some detailed directions to each farm and residence of those mentioned in the report, but no photos of the farms or the houses they lived in. Any photos of the houses would have been beneficial to me. From my dream, grandfather showed me a specific house, and it was my belief once I found this house, I would also find Dan Minuex. Thinking about the house from my dream, I once again pictured it in my mind. The two-story Victorian house was in the country and not in a town. My gut instinct was now telling me it was in Lane County, Kansas. The house was painted in a light brown color that reminded me of sand. The roof shingles were red, and the roof extended into an overhang that covered a large front porch. Handwritten at the bottom of page six was a single note that said, "All surveillance in Lane County ended on April 22nd, 1977." The FBI stopped looking for Minuex a whole month before Isabella's and Laney's deaths. Running that through my mind, I thought that it looked as if Minuex knew his friends and relatives were under surveillance, and he stayed out of sight. I could not blame the FBI agents involved, for it had to be difficult to keep watch on these farms and houses in the flattest country around, where you would stick out like a sore thumb. Also, all the locals would either be kin or friends of kin. All the locals would know you didn't belong. In my mind, once Minuex realized the FBI had abandoned the search for him, is when he made his plans to exact his revenge on Laney and Isabella. I had to hand it to the radical, for he had the wherewithal to sit it out and wait until the lion got bored and moved on. I had an advantage over those agents who spent all those days and hours trying to find Minuex. Grandfather had shown me in the dream the house where Minuex laid his head at night. All I had to do was find that house.

CHAPTER 28

The next two days I got myself prepared to make the trip to Kansas. According to my latest Rand McNally Road Atlas, Dighton, Kansas was roughly 400 miles away and would only take me about six hours to make the trip. First order of business was that I took my red 1974 Toyota Land Cruiser out of the garage and had the oil changed. Since I always drove the Grand County Sheriff Department's Chevy Blazer, my Land Cruiser had low mileage and even less wear and tear on it. My cruiser was bright red and would stick out, but I had already decided there was not any chance of doing this trip to stealthily find Minuex and that I was going to have to hide in plain sight.

Feeling like I needed to hear a little Cash as I cleaned my weapons, I thumbed through my older albums and found one of my dad's favorites titled "The Fabulous Johnny Cash." Some never considered Cash a great or even a talented singer, but his voice was timeless. His sound was unforgettable, an unmistakable bass-baritone voice, a flexible blend of country, rock 'n' roll, and folk music. The first song was an oldie, but goodie as they say – "Don't Take Your Guns to Town."

I can shoot as quick and straight as anybody can,
But I wouldn't shoot without a cause

WHEN THE SONG VANISHES

I listened to Johnny and then some Waylon Jennings as I cleaned my 357 Ruger Blackhawk and Ruger M-14. After that chore, I grabbed two boxes of ammo for each and then placed the guns and ammo by the front door so I would not forget them.

Remembering the conversation I had with Sheriff Tom Walker this morning, I knew he was not happy with my decision to take two weeks off. Not that I didn't have it coming or that I needed it. He knew without me telling him I was going hunting for Dan Minuex. When asked that very question, I didn't lie to him; I just didn't answer the question. I also told him that Nickey needed the same time off. My plan was to have her fly to her mother's place in Phoenix, Arizona until this ordeal with Minuex was over. I had not told her that was my plan yet, and I knew she would give me hell.

Nickey that evening made one of my favorites of hers - pork tamales. As we sat down to dinner, I informed her of my plan to leave in the morning to go to Kansas. I explained I would drop her off at the Stapleton Airport in Denver so she could catch a flight to Phoenix. After hearing of my plan, she stopped eating and stared at me, and I could see her anger raising. "Dane Lee, shame on you. Making a life and death decision without my input. Well, mister, that is total bullshit!"

"I need to keep you safe, Nickey and out of harm's way. You need to go to your mother's place in case Minuex has already started for here to complete his revenge. I can't stop thinking we may just pass each other on the highway with him headed here, and me headed there. You need to be someplace safe."

Nickey slammed her fork down and said, "And who keeps you safe? Nobody in Timbuktu, Kansas is going to have your back. We are better off as a team, and recent history with the Insurgence proves that. I am going with!"

I was getting angry, and I never get angry at Nickey. "No Nickey, you're not going to Kansas. No way, no how! And that is final!"

*

The next morning as the Land Cruiser was eastbound on Interstate 70 and passing the exit sign to Stapleton Airport, I asked, "*Mi Vida*, how far is it to our next exit in Limon, Colorado?"

As Nickey got the road atlas out, she turned and smiled that cocky little smile of hers. She knew full well I could never tell her no if she put some effort in to get her way. I finally relented and said she could go at 1:00 a.m. this morning.

Nickey studied the map and replied, "Looks to me to be about seventy-five to eighty miles to exit 363 onto US-287 south toward Hugo and Kit Carson."

We got gas for the Toyota in Limon, which was the home of the "Badgers," the local high school mascot according to more than a half a dozen signs we drove by before and on the way out of town. As I headed southeast toward Hugo, the surrounding countryside was not what I was used to. Flat pastureland was as far as the eye could see north, east, and south. The Rocky Mountains to the west were just a faded blue vista that was shimmering in the heat of the day on the distant horizon.

The day had become hot and dry as the sun made its arc across a cloudless sky. It seemed we were in the land of the tumbleweeds. The wind out of the north brought them to life as they rolled across the highway in front of us, scattering their seeds as nature intended. Just like cowboys, wagon trains, and buffalo, tumbleweeds were and still are icons of the Old West. These twisted balls of dead foliage rolling across the open range are staples of Western movies and the American imagination. The sound they made was a surreal screech as they occasionally crashed into the side of the Land Cruiser in a death roll.
After driving through Hugo and then several miles to the right, we passed the "blink once and they are gone" tiny towns of Boyero, Aroya, and the Colorado eastern plains ghost town of Wild Horse listening to Bob Seger's "Beautiful Loser." My favorite song on that tape was "Travelin' Man."

WHEN THE SONG VANISHES

Leaving my home, leaving my friends,
Running when things get too crazy
Out to the road, out 'neath the stars,
Feeling the breeze, passin' the cars

The road was isolated and lonely, and we only passed two pickups as we continued toward Kit Carson. Nickey and I had been quiet sticking to our own thoughts when she turned down the volume of the tape player and radio. "So, if the country around Dighton is anything like it is here, this bright red Land Cruiser is going to stick out like a flashing red light. What's our story going to be when we go snooping around?"

"Been thinking about that very thing. We both know about horses and would pass any inquisitive questioning about that subject. So, I think our cover story is we are looking to buy a small ranch to raise horses and maybe a few head of cattle. That way we can travel about the county looking for the so-called right opportunity as we check out the places where Minuex may be hiding."

Nickey nodded her head as she thought about that. "That actually might work. What if someone asks why we picked Lane County, Kansas?"

Nickey had a good point, and I thought about that for a minute before answering, "We make it simple. We say we heard land prices were cheaper in Lane County than most places."

"Is that true?" Nickey asked.

Laughing, "I do not know, **Mi Vida**. If they ask questions like that, just blink those pretty eyes and flash that beautiful smile, and nobody is going to give a shit why we are there."
After Nickey got done laughing, her face turned serious. "Are we crazy to be doing this?"

Reaching out my right hand, I slowly massaged Nickey's leg and responded, "I think it is what we need to do to stay alive. Minuex has shown his true colors and will be relentless in his pursuit of revenge. I know the man will come looking for us sooner than later. Grandfather told me to take the fight to him in my dream, and that is what we are going to do. In reality, Minuex is not that much different from me. I'm a fighter. I believe in the eye-for-an-eye business. I'm no cheek turner. I got no respect for a man who won't hit back. You kill my dog, you better hide your cat. This is who I am. And if you look in the mirror my love, it is who you are."

Nickey slowly nodded her head as we approached Kit Carson, Colorado and said, "Hate to admit it, but it is true. Let's go get the bastard!"

Kit Carson was a historic town named after the famous American frontiersman Christopher Houston Carson, better known as Kit Carson. He was a fur trapper, wilderness guide, Indian agent, and U.S. Army officer. He became a frontier legend in his own lifetime by biographies and news articles, and exaggerated versions of his exploits were the subject of dime novels. His understated nature belied confirmed reports of his fearlessness, combat skills, tenacity, and profound effect on the westward expansion of the United States.

After driving through Kit Carson, highway 287 turned due south and headed to Eads, Colorado. The next twenty miles between Kit Carson and Eads was just as desolate except for the rolling tumbleweeds we encountered. Just south of Eads, we turned eastward onto Highway 96, which would take us straight into Dighton, Kansas.

Just a few miles outside of Eads, we passed a sign stating that the Sand Creek Massacre site was ahead. After asking about the sign, I explained to Nickey the significance of it. The Sand Creek massacre also known as the Chivington massacre, or the battle of Sand Creek, was a one–sided massacre of Cheyenne and Arapaho Indians by the U.S. Army during the American Indian Wars. The carnage occurred on November 29, 1864 when a 675-man force of the Third Colorado Cavalry under the command of U.S. Volunteers Colonel John Chivington attacked and destroyed a village of Cheyenne and Arapaho killing over 150 of the tribes, most of whom were women and children. As we drove past the road that headed north to the massacre site on the banks of Sand Creek, I could feel my own Ute Indian heritage tugging at my soul with the pain and misery of those who had died so many years ago. One of these days, I would have to make a trip back here.

Nickey had plugged into the cassette player one of her favorite tapes, "Agents of Fortune" by the band Blue Oyster Cult. The song that was playing was "Don't Fear the Reaper."

All our times have come here,
But now they're gone,
Seasons don't fear the reaper,
Nor do the wind,
The sun or the rain

The next forty miles before the Colorado and Kansas border were filled with a dusty highway, tumbleweeds, and the small, almost forgotten towns of Chivington, Brandon, Sheridan Lake, and Towner.

Just as we passed the "Welcome to Kansas" sign, the terrain changed from strictly pastureland to actual farm ground with more farms along the highway as we passed the towns of Tribune, Selkirk, and headed into Leoti. In Leoti we stopped and filled up the Toyota's gas tank and got a bite to eat just off Main Street in Reifschneider Rexall drug store where they had a lunch counter. Pulling out of Leoti, we finally saw a sign that said Scott City twenty-four miles and Dighton forty-eight miles. Less than an hour later, we slowed down as we hit the outskirts of the town of Dighton.

CHAPTER 29

Dighton, Kansas was even smaller than I had imagined. It took us five minutes to drive eastbound from one end of town to the other on Highway 96. Folks seemed friendly enough as we passed them, and they gave Nickey and me the raised two-finger salute off their steering wheels in the common Midwestern greeting to say "howdy." We passed a small grocery store named Newsome IGA and a few blocks later we passed what looked like a convenience store called the Dart-In. The busiest place on this hot day seemed to be a hamburger and ice cream stand called the Frigid Crème. On the east side of town, pulling into the parking lot of the John Deere tractor dealership, I stopped the Land Cruiser and asked, "Well Nickey, what do you think?"

Nickey chuckled slightly. "Dighton does not seem like the hotbed of radical idealism to me. Seems more like a town you drive through on the way to someplace else and never really think twice about it."

Not sure what I was expecting, but Dighton seemed just like any other small town that I had ever encountered, full of hardworking folks. "I agree with you, Dighton is very unassuming. We need to find a place to stay, and I only saw a couple of places - the Dighton Hotel and the Chapel Lane Motel. Which would you prefer?"

"Let's see if they have a room at the Chapel Lane Motel. Sounds sort of peaceful."

The more I thought about it, the motel was a more ideal place to stay; more than likely we could park right in front of the room and could keep an eye on the Land Cruiser better. "Chapel Lane it is then."

In less than ten minutes, we had our room at the Chapel Lane Motel. The office manager was a pretty, blonde teenage girl named Lisa Messenger. When I asked if they had a room available, she laughed, "All twelve rooms are available. It seems you are the only ones traveling today. How long do you plan on staying with us?"

Time to spin our cover story. "At least a week. We are looking to buy some ranch and farm ground around here to raise horses and some cattle."

Lisa's expression showed confusion as if to ask, "Why would anyone want to move here on purpose?" However, if she had any thoughts on it, she kept them to herself as she handed us the key to our room after I paid her in cash for a week's stay.

The Chapel Lane Motel was small with a dozen rooms. The building itself was one story and was built into an "L" shape with a stucco like finish that was painted baby blue. We had room 103, and the room was small and stuffy as I turned on the window air conditioner. The room was barely functional, but spotless. There was a small bathroom with a tub and shower: one queen-size bed; one small dresser; one ancient television; one kitchen type table; two chairs; a microwave; and a small fridge. The interior walls were 8 x 16 cinderblocks that were painted white. Once we had moved our suitcases, weapons, and the FBI folder that Ken had given us into the room, the window AC had already cooled the room and refreshed the air. Spreading the file on the kitchen table, I opened it up, and Nickey and I both started studying it, trying to come up with a plan on how we were going to do our surveillance. We had already passed the tiny town of Amy, which was roughly seven miles west of Dighton off Highway 96. There was not much there - a small school, grain elevator, and a few houses. Since we were limited on time, Nickey and I decided not to waste any time and decided this afternoon to go look up an old friend and classmate of Minuex, a wheat farmer named John Lynch.

Using the phone book from the motel room, I found a phone number and an address for Lynch in Amy. Apparently, his farm was north of the small town on county road 160 that ran east and west. Unfolding the map of Lane County that I had brought with me, I found the road that the Lynch farm was on.

After looking at the Lane County map, Nickey sighed loudly and I asked, "What's bothering you, *Mi Vida*?"

"When we decided to make this trip, it seemed like a brilliant plan, but now that we are here, I realize what a daunting task this really is. Now I am wondering if we are wasting our time. We and the Land Cruiser stick out like a sore thumb. Also, we have no real time training in surveillance. We have five probable locations and not enough time to properly watch them even if we knew exactly what we were doing…which we don't."

Grabbing Nickey's hand, I sat her down and looked her in the eye. "As always, Nickey, you are absolutely correct. The difference is even though we don't have training in FBI surveillance, it doesn't matter because we do not have to spend a lot of time at each location. We have an advantage that the FBI never had; we know exactly what house we are looking for. Grandfather showed it to me, and the image is burned in my memory. All we must do is drive out there and make a couple of passes looking for that specific house from my dream. We are looking for a two-story Victorian house painted in a light brown color that looks like sand. The roof shingles will be red, and the roof will extend into an overhang that covered a large front porch. We just stick to our cover story until we locate that house."

Nickey still looked concerned. "You are that confident that is the house where we will find him? A house from a dream?"

"I am. That house is where Dan Minuex is hiding. Grandfather's dreams have never been wrong; it just takes me time to understand them is all. I believe in the dream, and I believe in grandfather."

Nickey's demeanor changed to one of more confidence as she spoke, "Dane, if you believe, then so do I."

Before leaving the room, Nickey and I made sure our weapons were fully loaded including the rifle. Hiding the pistols and the rifle in duffel bags, we loaded them, spare ammo, field glasses, and ourselves into the Land Cruiser.

The town of Amy, Kansas had a large grain elevator and in the shadow of it was a Baptist Church and a nice-looking white house right next to the church. Directly across on the other side of Highway 96 was a small, red and brown brick school. John Lynch's farm was easy to locate once we found county road 160 north of Amy. He had a huge white mailbox at the road entrance to his farm with J. Lynch painted in black on the side.

The afternoon was sultry with no clouds in the sky, and county road 160 was dirt and gravel and we were kicking up a dust cloud behind us as we traveled down the road. Even if we had tried to hide, there was no possibility of it; we could be seen for miles in all directions in this flat farm country. I drove by the farm heading westbound, and the main house and a few outbuildings, including a barn, were just one quarter mile north of the county road. After a mile of driving west, I pulled a U-turn and headed back east down the road we had just traveled to have another look see at the farm. Once I came upon the entrance to the farm, I stopped and took out the binoculars and looked at the main house, but nothing on this farm resembled my dream. The house was a small one-story ranch style house that was painted white as were all the other buildings except the barn, which was painted red. Dropping the binoculars and letting them hang from the strap on my neck, I turned to Nickey in the passenger seat and said, "Not even close to the dream; Minuex is not here, never has been."

As the day wound down, the sun was dropping below the western horizon. Seemed odd to me to look west and see no mountains, just a flat line in the distance. Only been gone for less than a day and was already missing home, but the sunsets were just as beautiful. The one that Nickey and I were now experiencing was as orange and blue as those in our mountains.

We stepped in at the motel hoping to find Lisa still at work; she was. Lisa pointed out that there were basically only two places to eat in Dighton - the Frigid Crème or the local bowling alley, Dighton Bowl. Lisa said both had excellent food, and if we were looking for more than just burgers that the Dighton bowling alley had more of the home cooking style. Nickey and I decided on the bowling alley.

Dighton Bowl was a small, blonde brick building, and the entrance faced east. Once we were inside, the restaurant was up front and the bowling alley with eight lanes was in the back. All eight lanes were busy as folks were either bowling or sitting in the white and turquoise chairs that were at the head of the bowling lanes. The restaurant was nothing fancy but clean, and the menu was to our liking. Our server, another pretty, blonde-haired gal named Colleen Hubin, took our order of meatloaf and mashed taters for me and fried chicken and mashed taters for Nickey.

After placing our order, I took more notice of the restaurant and of those that were eating. Someone had tiled the floor in alternating black and white. The owners had covered the walls with old vintage signs, such as Gulf Oil, Chevrolet, railroad crossing, and many others. Behind the cashier was a television mounted up high surrounded by many old black and white photos of cattle, horses, farms, and such. There was no outward display of the radical ideology of the Posse Comitatus or the Insurgence displayed anywhere in the room.

The folks gathered here eating were of course interested in us since we were not locals, and they now and then glanced our way, trying to place us. Most of the older men were dressed in blue jean bibs and the younger men mostly just in blue jeans. Each man was wearing a ball cap of some sort. The women wore mostly loose-fitting sun dresses. Nothing seemed out of place or unusual. Just as Colleen had placed our food on the table, Nickey said, "Oh Shit!"

I almost laughed out loud as I was looking at her chicken. "What? Chicken looks great, I will trade you."

Looking up, I could see Nickey staring behind me. "What is it?"

Nickey's eyes now caught mine. "Turn around slowly and look at the television above the cashier."

Slowly I turned as not to draw any attention, and I saw what she had seen, "Oh Shit!"

On the television, the local news station was playing an old news clip of Nickey being interviewed during the time when the manhunt for Minuex was in full operation in Rocky Mountain National Park. The caption below simply said, "GRAND COUNTY DEPUTY NICKEY LEE."

CHAPTER 30

After seeing Nickey on the tube, I glanced around the room and no one in the restaurant part of the bowling alley had been looking at the television. They were all busy talking to one another or eating their meals. It would seem none of them had realized that the lady on the TV and the one sitting at my table were the same. Looking back at Nickey, I saw a look of horror on her face, and I suddenly found it comical and started to laugh. Leaning across the table, I said quietly, "Not one person was looking at the television when you were on. Nobody noticed. I sort of feel sorry for them all, missing the most beautiful woman in Colorado and Kansas." Nickey rolled her eyes at my comment, "Just in Colorado and Kansas?"

"I don't get out much. There might be a more gorgeous gal in Texas or South Dakota. I just never been there to compare is all. So, for now just Colorado and Kansas."

That brought a smile to *Mi Vida's* face. "I am going to keep my cowboy slash Indian close to home so he doesn't feel the need to go looking elsewhere."

WHEN THE SONG VANISHES

Sitting back in my chair, "You know at the motel, I registered us under our actual names. Never even thought about saying anything different."

It was Nickey's turn to laugh out loud, "A couple of amateur sleuths we are. A real Abbott and Costello combo."

"If there was another one of us, we could be the three stooges."

After supper, Nickey and I both agreed that the food was excellent. My meatloaf was some of the best I had ever eaten. The cashier turned out to be the owner of the Dighton Bowl. Being new in town, he introduced himself as Mike Magee, the proud owner of the bowling alley. Mike was an older man wearing an orange and black Dighton Hornets ball cap, the mascot of the local high school. Mike was about 5'8", slender, and talkative. He was obviously curious about Nickey and me. "Never seen you folks around town before. Whatcha doing in the metropolitan of high dining in Dighton?"

No use trying to come up with different names, so I introduced us, "Glad to meet you Mike, this is my lovely wife Nickey and my name is Dane. We are in town for a few days looking to possibly buy a small farm and ranch hereabouts and get our feet wet and raise a few cows and horses."

Mike sort of nodded his head up and down as he ran that statement through his thinker. "Do you know anything about farming or ranching?"

"Not really. We know horses, but that is about the extent of our knowledge. That is why we are hoping to start small and work ourselves up."

That brought a chuckle from the owner, "Well, most of the farmers and ranchers around here don't have a clue about farming or ranching either. You would fit right in."

Mike then pointed through the front glass window and said, "Is that there a foreign type job?"

My gaze followed along his pointed finger, and I realized he meant our Land Cruiser. "If you mean foreign made, that would be a yes. That is a 1974 Toyota Land Cruiser. I bought it brand new off the showroom floor in Denver."

"Toyota? That's a Jap name, isn't it?"

Mike had said that as if he had disapproved of our vehicle choice. "Yes, it is Japanese. I bought it because we now live in the Colorado Mountains, and we need a good 4 x 4 and some folks there swear by them."

"Some folks in these parts might call that unpatriotic - you know; be American, buy American sort of thing. Not me personally, but some would around here. Personally, I think it is funny and call crapola on it?"

Not sure where this conversation was going, I said, "Find what funny?"

"Think about it, son. World War II, we bombed every stinking bridge, railroad, train, and factory in Germany. In Japan we dropped not one, but two atomic bombs on their asses to win the war. Thirty years later they are getting their revenge by low balling those Detroit carmakers by selling us low-priced cars and trucks. Don't get me wrong, I think those Krauts and Japs make suitable vehicles; I just find it somewhat humorous is all."

Mike gave us our change and said he hoped to see us soon and mentioned that the Dighton Bowl was open at seven a.m. for breakfast. Once outside Nickey said, "Felt like he was giving us crap about the Toyota, but in a nice way."

I replied with a chuckle, "He was! The way he said Krauts and Japs, I am surprised he didn't start on me for being Indian."

WHEN THE SONG VANISHES

Once we were back at the motel, Nickey and I laid out the Lane County map again and with the local telephone book, we plotted out our day for tomorrow. We decided to head to Healy right after breakfast, then to Shields, and finish out the day back here in Dighton at Dan Minuex's uncle's farm.

When Nickey was taking her shower, I revisited the FBI folder that Ken had given us and reread about those potential hiding places for Dan Minuex in the towns of Healy, Shields, and Dighton. The descriptions were short and sweet without a lot of extra information.

There were two possible hideouts near Healy, Kansas. One was a wheat, milo, and alfalfa farmer named Bryan Cherry, a first cousin to the Minuex's and a known member of Posse Comitatus. The second possible connection was a man named Eric Sanders who, according to the report, was a close high school friend of Dan. Sanders actually lived in the town of Healy and was a tractor and auto mechanic there. He was not a known member of the Posse Comitatus. I was already dismissing him in my mind since it appeared he lived in the town of Healy, and in my dreams, the Victorian house was in the country. Since we were going to be in Healy anyway, we would check out his house as well.

In Shields, Kansas lived Bart and Brett Chipman; they were twins who operated the grain elevator in Shields. They were not known members of the Posse Comitatus but were close friends of the Minuex brothers in high school. According to the map and the addresses, I could not determine where their houses were exactly. They could be in town or in the country. Both had to be checked out.

Just south of Dighton is where the uncles of Dan and Mitch farmed. Their names were Harvey and Rip Minuex, known members of the Posse Comitatus. They were wheat, alfalfa, and milo farmers. It appeared they both lived in different houses, but on the same farm.

Nickey finished her shower, and she didn't even bother to put on those lace panties I liked so well. Making love to my wife was no doubt my favorite pastime. One hour later after we both were exhausted from making love and when we were bathed in each other's aroma, Nickey rolled on to her side and closed her eyes. It was only a few seconds, and she was breathing easily and sound asleep. Watching her sleep in the half-light of the waning moon that peaked in through almost transparent curtains of our room, I realized once again what a lucky man I was.

Once on my back, I watched the ceiling fan as it rotated in a blur, listening to the sounds of an occasional car or truck that passed the motel on Highway 96. Clearing my mind, I thought about our task of our so-called surveillance tomorrow. It was simple really; we just had to find the house from my grandfather's dream. My gut instinct told me the old Victorian house was here in Lane County, somewhere close. I knew Minuex would be there; it was his lair. It is where he rested before moving out from the shadows to wreak havoc against those whom he saw as his enemy. Real or imagined, Dan Minuex had a lot of enemies. Once we find the radical's hideout, then it was no longer a simple matter. Dan Minuex was a dangerous and unpredictable man., skilled in the way of warfare and no stranger in dealing out death. I can only imagine the horrors the man saw during his tours in Vietnam. Whatever happened there in those steamy jungles obviously changed the man into what he was today. Was he insane? Maybe. If I had just heard his story and was not personally involved, I would have sympathy for him and his causes. But given the circumstances, Dan Minuex needed to die for what he did in Grand County and in Nashville, Tennessee. Reaching my hand out, I lay it gently on Nickey's naked hip and hoped and prayed that in the process of the righteous justice that needed to be served that I didn't get Nickey and me killed.

CHAPTER 31

After visiting the Dighton Bowl the following morning for a breakfast of eggs, toast, and bacon, Nickey and I headed to Healy. The town of Healy was seventeen miles northwest of Dighton. We headed north on highway 23 until it slowly rolled westward onto Kansas 4, and twenty minutes later we passed a "Welcome to Healy, Home of the Eagles" sign. By the looks of it, Healy was a small town, even smaller than Dighton.

We were able to locate the tractor and auto mechanic Eric Sanders' house and shop in town. According to the FBI report, Sanders had been a close friend of Dan Minuex. Just as I had thought it would be, the house that Sanders lived in was not the house from my grandfather's dreams. It was a small ranch-style house built into an "L" shape and painted sky blue, which was the same color as the mechanic shop next to the house. Dismissing Sanders' house as a hideout for our radical fugitive, I pulled over to the side of the road and looked at the Lane County map.

According to the map, Bryan Cherry's farm was a mile north and a mile west of Healy. We headed north on Dodge Road until we located County Road 240. Before heading west toward the farm of the known member of the Posse Comitatus, I pulled over to the side of the gravel and white rock road. Nickey and I, without talking or hesitation, got ready our weapons and made sure they were fully loaded. Cherry, according to the FBI report, was a first cousin of the Minuex's. Being kin was always a powerful connection, especially when you shared the same radical views of the world. Bryan Cherry could be a very dangerous man.

The northern Kansas sky was turning dark as a storm made its way slowly in our direction. Hard to tell how long before or even if that storm was going to make our tasks a tad tougher today. Looking at my wife, I asked, "Are you ready?"

Nickey, always the trooper, nodded her head yes and replied, "Ready as I will ever be. Let's go check out Mr. Cherry's farm."

A quarter mile westward down County Road 240 there was an older two-tone brown and white Dodge pickup half on the road and half in the drainage ditch with the driver's door wide open. There was a sour looking, dark-haired man standing next to the truck eyeballing three Hereford cows that were without a care in the world grazing in the ditch. Apparently, they had gotten out of the pasture and the man was attempting to get them back in. As I slowed down the Land Cruiser, Nickey asked, "What do you think?"

"Thinking it would be the natural and friendly thing to do is to ask if he needs help."

Stopping the Toyota on the road next to the rancher's truck, I told Nickey, "Stay in the Land Cruiser and keep your weapon at ready. I am going to go see if I can be of help."

As I got out of the Toyota on the opposite side away from the rancher, I pulled my long-tailed shirt out of the top of my pants and placed my 357 Ruger Blackhawk in the small of my back, hiding it with my loose-fitting shirt. As I did this, Nickey hand-cranked her window down and asked, "Did your cows get out?"

The man looked at our license plate then back at Nickey. "Isn't that obvious, even to someone from Colorado?"

Stepping around from the front of the Toyota, I said, "Just trying to be friendly is all. Do you need a hand getting them back in?"

The man took a few steps toward me and then stopped; he was eyeballing me something fierce. He looked to be in his late forties, six feet tall, muscular, and with dark, shaggy hair that failed to see a comb this morning. The disgruntled rancher had a good four or five days' growth of beard. Once the man had taken a good look at me, he asked, "What's your business here, boy?"

"At the moment, we are just trying to be friendly and offer a hand, but if you don't need it, we will be on our way."

The rancher kept staring at my face as if he was trying to place me before saying, "I sure as hell don't need help from any government pukes or your lady friend. I thought all you FBI punks had left Lane County."

"If you don't want our help, then I guess we will take our leave then."

Just as I said that, a smile slowly crept across the face of the rancher. "Wait a minute! Now that I got a good look at you, I know who you are. I also recognize the woman. Seen both of you on the television, and neither of you are with the FBI! You're the assholes that shot up my cousins - the Minuex's boys - and their friends. Hell, I am almost shaking in my boots being around some tough hombres such as yourselves. Your name is… give me a second… your name is Lee, Dane Lee. And the woman's name is Nickey, I believe. You're the law dogs from Grand County, Colorado. What happened, you get lost? You are about 300 miles off your range, boy! You ain't got jurisdiction here, not you, not her! What the hell are you doing here in Lane County?"

Just our luck to run into Bryan Cherry on the road and for him to recognize us for who we really are. It would seem in less than twenty-four hours we had blown any type of cover story we thought we had. Might as well not even pretend anymore about looking for a farm or ranch to buy. Bryan Cherry, a known member of the Posse Comitatus, was right about one thing, and that was Nickey and I were way out of our jurisdiction. Hell, we were even in the wrong state.

I could see the anger and the hate in the radical farmer. Sizing the farmer up now, I could see that this conversation was quickly deteriorating into a possible physical confrontation that I did not need. Cherry looked like a man that was hardened by a lifetime of physical labor and more than likely was as tough as he looked. He seemed to be unarmed, but I would guess that he had a firearm or two in his pickup. The radical had asked a question, and I needed to answer it and show no back up in doing so. "We are looking for your cousin Dan Minuex. You, being a first cousin of the wanted fugitive, we thought we would drive down the road and use my binoculars to take a look-see at your place."

Cherry stared hard at me for several seconds before he chuckled, "Guess, you ain't heard law dog, but according to the FBI my cousin is dead. Supposedly a rotting corpse in those mountains you call home, and his body is the proper makings for some mountain lion or a brown bear's shit. Even if the SOB was still alive, he would never come to my place. He never cottoned to me much, and truth be told, I didn't like him much either. So, go ahead and take your look-see. You don't even need any fancy binoculars to do so. Drive on down to the farm, house is open. Do what you need to do but steal nothing. Once you are done, then get the hell off my land and don't come back. I might not be so accommodating next time."

Slowly backing away from Bryan Cherry until I got behind the Land Cruiser, I then climbed into the driver's seat. Making sure Nickey was still monitoring Cherry, I pulled out and headed westward toward the Cherry farm. Once we were far enough away from Bryan Cherry, Nickey laughed then said, "That went well." That made me laugh, and I replied, "I hope his cows get hit by a freakin' speeding semi-truck."

A minute later we were sitting on the county road, not wanting to drive onto the disgruntled farmer's property, looking through the binoculars at Bryan Cherry's house...or rather, his shitty mobile home he lived in. It took me all of ten seconds to realize that what I was looking at was not even close to the house I saw in the dream with my grandfather. The mobile home needed paint and did not look level, and the front porch was a mess of rotting wood; the mobile home probably needed many other repairs. I could only imagine the filth inside such a home. Shaking my head no, I told Nickey, "This morning has been crap - cover completely blown and that house is not the house we are looking for. Once Cherry gets to a phone today, everyone in Lane County will know we are here not looking for land but looking for Dan Minuex...including Dan Minuex if he is still alive. Taking the Insurgence member by surprise is not an option now, if it was ever an option."

Once satisfied that Bryan Cherry's house was not the hideout for Minuex, I turned the Land Cruiser around and drove eastward slowly passing Cherry as he was still trying to get his runaway cows back into the pasture. Cherry saw us coming and put his hands on his hips and gave us the ole' stink eye as we rolled past him.

I wanted to flip him my middle finger but reluctantly refrained from doing so, but not Nickey, she clenched her teeth as she gave him the bird.

CHAPTER 32

Heading back eastward on the highway toward Healy on Kansas 4, I stopped the Toyota on the side of the road. The Lane County road map proved useful again and indicated that the town of Shields was straight ahead on Highway 4. By the looks of it, probably only seven or eight miles away.

Nickey had already pulled out and started reviewing the FBI folder that Ken had given us and read out loud, "Bart and Brett Chipman, twins who operate the grain elevator in Shields. Not known members of the Posse Comitatus. Close friends of the Minuex brothers in high school."

One old farm truck passed us heading west, but other than that there were no other vehicles on the road and ten minutes later we passed a sign which said, "Shields welcomes you." The tallest thing in Shields was a tall white grain elevator which we stopped in front of. In black letters Shields was painted on the elevator, and the one-story building sitting in front of it had the name "Chipman Ent" also painted in black letters. Looking at the Lane County map and the Lane County phone book, we could not determine whether the twins were living in town or out in the country some place close. Nickey looked at me and said, "What do you think?"

Rolling my eyes and chuckling, I said, "Well since our cover is already shot to hell, thinking we just go inside the office and ask to see if the twins are in."

"Then what?" Nickey asked.

"I guess, play it by ear on what we learn."

Nickey and I both tucked our service pistols in the top of our pants with the grips above our belts, and then we pulled our shirts out and let them hang loose to hide the fact that we were packing. Once inside the office, the only person that could be seen was a heavy-set older woman sitting at a desk filling out some form. Once we were standing at the counter, she looked up and smiled and asked, "Can I help you?"

Speaking with authority that I did not have in Kansas, "Yes, is Bart or Brett here?"

"No, they are not in at the moment; is there something I can help you with?"

Thinking on that for a second, I inquired, "Is it possible you can give us directions to where they live? We could run by and see if they are home."

The woman chuckled, "You would have to drive to Dighton to see them. They both have lady friends there and spend considerable time in Dighton. Not sure where in town the gals live."

Running that information through my thinker, "Actually we are more interested in seeing their houses than seeing them, could you help us with that?"

The smile faded on the older woman's face and with a voice of caution, she asked, "Why?"

Since our cover was blown, I decided to tell the truth. "We are law enforcement from Colorado, and we are looking for Dan Minuex. We have reason to believe that Mr. Minuex may be staying at one of their houses. We have a description of the house but not the whereabouts, and we would like to check out the exterior of their houses to see if one of their houses matches the description we have."

A look of total confusion passed quickly over the woman's face, and then it was replaced with a smirk, "Word here is that Dan died in Colorado. And the description of the so-called house must be a wild goose chase. But, since you are here and you asked, I will do you one better. I will even let you have a look inside where the twins live."

"We actually just need to see the outside, and we won't bother you about letting us inside."

The woman now started to laugh out loud, "Well Mr. and Mrs. Law Enforcement from Colorado, it is no trouble at all. Bart and Brett being single and of the courting age, live in rooms in the back of this office. Just by standing here, you are in their house. Whoever gave you that description of the house must be laughing their asses off."

Once Nickey and I both were back in the Toyota, we started laughing with Nickey saying, "Well, that was easy enough to scratch those two names off the list."

The storm and dark clouds that had been building in the north were moving closer, and we could see a few lingering lightning flashes even from the distance. Nickey was watching the storm and said, "How far away do you think the storm is? Looks nasty from here?" Following my wife's gaze, I answered, "Not sure. In the mountains, I could give you a good guess. Here in this flatland, I have trouble gauging distance. My best guess, the storm is moving slowly and seems to me to be about forty or so miles away. If it does not peter out, I suspect the rainstorm will be here sometime tonight. It isn't even noon yet, which gives us plenty of time to check out the two other possible hideouts before dark."

Nickey pulled out the FBI file on the Insurgence and read the next entry, "Irvin Maddox, known member of the Posse Comitatus. Cattle rancher and wheat farmer. Ex-brother-in-law of the Minuex brothers. Lives just south of Alamota, Kansas."

Unfolding the Lane County map and after cross checking it with the address in the Lane County phone book, I said, "Looks to me as if we need to head back to Dighton and then east on Highway 96 for about nine miles and then a mile south to Alamota. Then south three miles from Alamota and then turn east on Road 110 one mile to the Maddox farm. Should take us half an hour to get there."

Once back in Dighton, the Frigid Crème was open, and we grabbed a couple of cheeseburgers and limeades to go and headed out to Alamota. Back on the road again with our burgers, I plugged in the Eagles' "Hotel California" cassette tape. The song "Life in the Fast Lane" started filling the Land Cruiser with a great tune.

They went rushin' down that freeway,
Messed around and got lost
They didn't care,
They were just dyin' to get off and it was
Life in the fast lane
Surely makes you lose your mind

Once we turned south from Highway 96, the road was a white rock road; a mile later we passed Alamota on the right, which was a tall, white grain elevator and a few houses. Once we located the Maddox farm on County Road 110, we were surprised to see that the house had recently burnt to the ground, making it obvious that Dan Minuex was not using the Maddox farm as his hideout.

Stopping the Toyota, Nickey read out loud the final and last entry in the FBI file about possible hideouts for Minuex, "Harvey and Rip Minuex, known members of the Posse Comitatus. Wheat, alfalfa, and milo farmers. Uncles of the Minuex brothers. It seems that both live on the same farm just south of Dighton. This has to be the farm where Minuex is hiding."

Once again, we referenced the Lane County Road map and phone book and headed back to Dighton. After the one and only traffic light in Dighton turned green, I took a left turn from Highway 96 on to Highway 23 and headed south two miles to county road 130. Once I turned east from the highway onto another white rock road, I stopped. Since Dan Minuex's uncle's farm was last on the FBI list, we felt this had to be the place where the old two-story Victorian house was located. Closing my eyes, I concentrated on what the old house looked like again from my dream. The house was painted in a light brown color, much like the color of sand. The roof shingles were red, and the roof extended into an overhang that covered a large front porch. Grandfather's warning inundated my thoughts, "Heed my words Dane, the one that got away is not done with you or the ones you love." The uncle's farm had to be where the radical was hiding out. The one who had killed Laney McKay and Isabella Edwards. The one who had a hand in the deaths of so many others whom I cared for. The death faces of Laney, Rod, Isabella, Barry, Zach, and John engulfed my mind. Until the day I die, uncertainties of my actions on that fateful night of our battle with the Insurgence would haunt me forever. Dan Minuex had to pay for what he had done. He would never see the inside of a prison cell if I had my way. He needed to bleed for those that I loved! Minuex needed to die!

Nickey and I both got out, and this time we belted on our holsters; we were confident that Minuex was hiding out just down the road a mile. Taking my Ruger M-14 rifle out of its scabbard, I checked to make sure it was fully loaded. After handing the rifle to Nickey, we got back into the Land Cruiser, and I spun the tires as I hit the gas; white rocks and white dust filled the air behind the Land Cruiser.

WHEN THE SONG VANISHES

The sun was still shining, but the dark, ominous clouds of the storm were slowly moving southward and encroaching upon Lane County. The clouds mirrored my mood; there was a reckoning upon the horizon.

We passed a small white sign stating that we were approaching Harvey and Rip Minuex's place. There was an American flag flying just above the sign. I hit the brakes so hard that Nickey almost slammed into the dash. Now that Harvey and Rip Minuex's farm was in full view, both Nickey and I stared in disbelief at the sprawling farm lain out before us. There were two houses of course - one for each of the uncles. Neither of them was an old two-story Victorian house! Not even close; both of them were white single story modular homes. The house from the dream was not here. Almost as if we had practiced it, Nickey and I both simultaneously said, "What the hell?"

CHAPTER 33

Nickey looked at me, and her face showed the confusion I felt. She said, "What now?"

Still in disbelief, "I don't have a clue. Grandfather's dreams have always panned out in one form or another. I have always relied on them to show me the way and the truth. The dreams were always like a sure bet. Not once have they ever been wrong. This may have been a mistake coming here."

Nickey reached out and gently touched my arm before she said, "We still have time here. Let's go back to Dighton and grab some supper and think about our next step."

Once again, I looked at the farmstead of Harvey and Rip Minuex, and nothing seemed like my grandfather's dream. Disappointed, I looked north at the approaching storm and the flashes of lightning mixed within the dark clouds and said, "Not sure what I expected, Nickey, but I never expected to come up empty-handed. You are right, let's go get something to eat and decide what to do next."

WHEN THE SONG VANISHES

I turned the Toyota around on the white gravel road and spun the tires spraying white rocks and dust as we headed back to Dighton. The feelings of defeat and frustration were overwhelming. The preparation and anticipation had been nerve wracking of what I thought would be a confrontation with the radical Insurgence member. We had come to the end of the list of possible hideouts with no Dan Minuex, no justice, and no end in sight. Felt like someone had hit me with a sledgehammer.

Nickey slid in our Tom T. Hall cassette and the song "Faster Horses (The Cowboy and the Poet)" played.

Well, I was disillusioned
If I say the least,
I grabbed him by the collar
And I jerked him to his feet

In twenty-five minutes, we were seated at the Dighton Bowling alley. Colleen was our server again, and as soon as we had sat down, she handed us our menus and asked, "Any luck finding Dan?"

Nickey's mouth dropped open as we both looked at Colleen in utter amazement. It was obvious that we were in a small town as the news of what we were really doing here had spread like wildfire. It appeared that the telephone system in Lane County worked like a charm. It was less than eight hours ago that we had our run in with Bryan Cherry. No need lying to the young girl, so I answered, "Not yet, but we still have time. Do you know where Mr. Minuex is?"

Colleen laughed a hearty laugh and with a big smile, "No, and I don't want to know. Dan and his brother were the scary type. Most people around here think he is dead, just like the newspapers said." Everyone in the diner part of the bowling alley was now looking at us. I asked Colleen, "What do you think? Do you think Dan is dead?"

Colleen's smile faded as she thought about my question before she answered, "Had not really thought about it much, but now you got me thinking. I don't think so. A man like Dan is tougher than all the others. He has a mean streak a mile wide and would be tough to kill. He is not the type to commit suicide like the papers said. No sir, I think he is very much alive."

Nickey and I both decided on meatloaf and once Colleen had our order, she headed off to the kitchen with it. Nickey and I sat in silence for several minutes. The television was on but muted above the cashier. You could hear the clash and crash of bowling pins being dropped by those that were bowling. All eight lanes were occupied. It would seem it was a league night. Everyone in the dining area kept glancing our way and then turned back toward the folks at their tables and spoke in hushed tones. Nickey noticed the reaction of the surrounding folks sitting at their tables and said, "It would seem everyone now knows who we are and what we are doing here. I think if Minuex was here hiding somewhere close, he would have gotten word of our presence and fled the area for parts unknown. What do you think?"

"Been thinking on that very subject. A man like Dan Minuex never ran from a fight unless it was obvious that he was at a tactical disadvantage. Here in Lane County, he definitely has the advantage. He knows the terrain, and he knows the people. If he is still alive, there is no way in hell he would have fled the area. He would hunt us down and then kill us."

Nickey's face went blank before she said, "I actually had not thought of that, but it makes sense. We need to sleep with our weapons at ready tonight. Dane, do you have any other pearls of wisdom that you would like to share?"
"I am also considering the possibility that Minuex is not here at all. After grandfather's dream and after reading the FBI file Ken gave us, I was positive he was here. The house in the dream was so vivid. My gut instinct told me so, but nothing I have seen today is even close to the house in the dream. I believe the house is real, but it just might not be here in Lane County. I know he is still alive

and that you and I are in mortal danger from the man. With all that has happened since the bank robbery in Grand Lake, I have made one mistake after another. People died because of those mistakes. If I had a chance to do it all over again, I would have done things differently. All the thought and preparation I had put into this trip seems to have been for naught. Almost embarrassing really. I am disappointed, and the cousin to disappointment is frustration. Frustration is the second storm. Very disillusioned, we hit a blank wall here, and now I am frustrated about what to do next."

My mind was lost in thought as I looked out through the glass window of the diner into the parking lot. The sun had yet to settle down for the day, and daylight still prevailed. The sun was not shining though as the dark and daunting clouds of the incoming storm were now overhead. As if to make a point, the Lord showed us who was in charge; the lights flickered four times in the Dighton bowling alley followed by a blinding flash of lightning lighting up the sky and the thunder rumbling in the distance. The storm that had been approaching all day was not on top of us just yet, but it was getting closer. Everyone now in the dining area was looking at the television as it flickered on and off. Once the lights came back on and stayed on, the owner of the bowling alley Mike Magee turned up the volume on the television. There was a map of Kansas, and there was a rolling warning at the bottom of the screen in a red background with bold white letters, "Severe thunderstorm warning with heavy rain mixed with hail for Lane County, Ness County, Gove County, Scott County, and Finney County until two a.m." Mike Magee turned to his diners and made an obvious observation as if he was the only one that could comprehend what the storm was doing. Mike said loudly enough for everyone to hear, "This storm is moving slowly if the severe weather watch is until two in the morning!"
I could hear Nickey mutter quietly under her breath, "No shit, Sherlock!"

That brought a smile to my face, and looking at her, "Be nice my love."

"I said it quietly. That guy's got an audience, and he loves being the bearer of bad news. I hate being around dipshits like that."

Now I laughed out loud, and everyone turned to look at us, giving me the stink eye as if I had brought the wrath of God and this storm down on their heads.

Now another warning rolled across the bottom of the screen and a new map of just western Kansas now appeared showing that two tornadoes had been spotted just south of Gove Kansas and north of Dighton. Nickey asked, "How close are the tornadoes?"

"From that map and what I can remember, I would say they are a good forty miles away from us. I do not believe those that are already on the ground are much of a danger for Dighton. Of course, that could change later as the storm gets closer."

After getting my belly full of some good home cooking, I felt better. Once we had gotten back to the motel, we would have to reevaluate what we knew at this point and then decide if we would stay a couple of extra days or head back home to Grand County. Nickey grabbed the check and left a five dollar tip on the table and headed toward the cashier and Mike Magee to pay our bill. I was right behind her. Being new to tornado country, Nickey started asking the owner many questions about tornadoes and such as I studied the old black and white photos on the wall next to the cash register. There were many photos of some old farmers and ranchers standing in a saloon. There were four or five photos of old farm equipment that were horse-drawn to thrash wheat back in the day.
Near the bottom of the photos on the wall, my eyes finally fell on a photo of a house sitting out in the country. My eyes drifted from it, and then I glanced back, for it felt familiar. The second glance brought even more curiosity. I looked hard at it, and I could not believe what I was seeing. I could not tell the color of the old two-story Victorian house because the photo was in sepia, but it had the large roof overhang over the front porch. The more I stared at the photo, I became convinced it was the same one in my grandfather's

dream. I rudely interrupted Nickey's and Mike's conversation and inquired about the photo and pointing at it, I said, "That photo, would you mind if I looked at it closer?"

The owner of the bowling alley seemed confused and looked at the photo on the wall. Then he reached for it and pulled the thumbtack out and handed it to me while speaking, "You mean this one?"

Nickey now was intrigued, and she looked hard at the photo I held in my hand and asked, "Dane, what is it?"

Ignoring Nickey, I asked Mike, "Do you know where this house is?"

Mike looked even more confused than Nickey, nodding his head yes. He said, "Of course I do. That is my grandparent's place in Pendennis, or rather was my grandparent's place. Bart and Brett Chipman own their old farm now."

Still looking at the photo, "Bart and Brett Chipman? The fellows that own the grain elevator in Shields?"

Nickey's face showed understanding when she asked Mike, "Pendennis? Is that a name of someone or is it a place?"

Mike still looking confused, "It is a small town or rather the remnants of a small town. Pendennis is six miles east of Shields. My grandparents' farm is another mile east of Pendennis on the north side of Highway 4. Why are you so interested in an old, abandoned farm?"

The more I studied the old sepia colored photo, I became even more convinced this was the house from my grandfather's dream. Nickey answered for me, "Oh, Dane just likes old Victorian style houses. They remind him of his grandparents' house. He takes photos of them and has a whole scrapbook of them at our house."

Nickey, still looking at Mike, started spinning her finger on the side of her head and with a chuckle said, "He is sort of a nut about them really, as you can tell."

Handing the photo back to the owner of the Dighton Bowl, "Yes, sorry, I find them fascinating. Thinking we might drive out there and take some photos for my scrapbook."

That seemed to satisfy Mike's curiosity, and he smiled when he said, "Once you pass Pendennis, you can't miss it. It is right on the highway and just a quarter mile north of the road. It is sort of sandy color with a bright red roof."

CHAPTER 34

Once seated in the Toyota, Nickey said, "Makes sense, we know the Chipman twins are friends of the Minuex's. It would seem they are letting Dan Minuex use their old house as a hideout. Obviously, the FBI is unaware that the house near Pendennis belonged to the twins, and it was never under surveillance. What is our next move?"

Starting the Land Cruiser, I replied, "Funny, I had never looked at those photos on the wall before. Tonight, while I was just buying time waiting on you to finish your conversation with Mike, there it was. We are going now. I don't want to lose him again!"

Daylight was coming to a finish as the light started to fade, and darkness of the night surrounded the Toyota. The rain had become heavier, and the huge rain drops carried a punch when they landed. Thick rain drops started pelting the Land Cruiser so hard that it sounded as if we were riding inside a drum. Occasionally, a soft and slushy hail would hit and then slowly melt on the windshield as an indicator of what was to come. Nickey looked concerned and said, "Are you sure you want to try this tonight?"

"I let Minuex slip through my fingers when I did not act fast enough on not finding the old moonshiner's cabin; I don't want to make that mistake again. The storm should give us cover on our approach. Yes, I think we should go after him tonight."

Through the rain, we could see lightning flash and then dance and then arc across the sky. The thunder was almost deafening as it descended from the heavens above us. Remembering the directions after passing through Shields and the description given to us by the owner of the bowling alley, I recollected we were getting close even though I could not see very well.

Nickey said, "By the mileage we should be here or at least close to the house in Pendennis."

After I stopped the Toyota, both Nickey and I glared out of the blurry rain-soaked windows to the north, trying to see anything. The storm was directly overhead and was furious in nature as it pelted us with lightning, thunder, and hammer-pounding rain. Just as I was about to give up for the night and seek shelter back in Dighton, a lightning bolt hit the white rock road about a mile ahead of us, and the crash of thunder followed immediately after the blinding flash. As my eyes quickly adjusted to the lingering flash, I saw it - the old Victorian house was sitting just a quarter mile off the road to the north just as Mike Magee had stated. That momentary light had given me a vision of what lay ahead. There it was, just like I saw it before in the dream. I recognized it for what it was – Minuex's hideout. My grandfather's dream had once again been spot on. The color of the house was light brown or as some would say, it was a sandy color. The roof shingles were red, and there was an extended overhang over a large front porch. Nickey, having also seen the house in the flash, exclaimed, "I will go to hell! Just like you described."
I reached behind me into the backseat and located two dark-colored raincoats with hoods we had brought with us from Colorado. I also grabbed Nickey's and my Grand County issued ballistic vests. Handing the smaller ones to Nickey, I said, "Each time one of my grandfather's dreams comes true, it even amazes me. You need to know if Minuex is not here and we go busting into that house, we are subject to arrest by local authorities. In fact, that could and probably would ruin our law enforcement careers.

WHEN THE SONG VANISHES

This is an enormous gamble, all on a dream. If you say no, then I will drive away and head back to Grand Lake. What do you think?"

Nickey pondered on what I had said for a full minute before answering, "Dane, if I didn't know you and had not seen for myself the results that the dreams you have about your grandfather, I would think this is all crazy. Your dreams and visions have never been wrong, not even once. I trust you with my life, and I trust this dream. The house is real. Dan Minuex being in that house, I believe, is real as well. If we don't bring a righteous justice and an end to this, Minuex will track us down and exact his revenge on us. We, as you have stated before, need to do this on our terms. Let's do this!"

Grabbing one of the M-14 rifles, I checked to see if it was loaded and then handed it to Nickey. Once I had the other M-14 in hand, I made sure my pistol was in its holster before I said, "You go east, and I will go west. As we approach the house, we need to stay within sight of each other in case one of us gets into trouble. Hopefully Minuex will be hunkered down out of the storm." I kissed *Mi Vida* with an enduring kiss, and then we both took a deep breath as we opened the Toyota's doors.

The wind was so robust it was difficult to open my door as the wind was pushing hard to shut it as I tried to open it. Nickey's door, on the other hand, was opposite of the wind and flew open and she almost hit the ground and the ever-deepening mud as she stumbled out of the Toyota.

Once I was out and standing in the mud, the wind slammed the Land Cruiser's door with a loud thump, and I feared the sound could be heard in the house. Then I realized the storm's howling wind and rolling thunder would cover all sounds that Nickey and I could ever make on this evening. The rain had not let up, and the drops were heavy and hard as they pummeled us. The hood of my rain slicker was flapping so hard and coupled with the rain created vision problems.

Nickey and I both fought the wind and stepped toward the front of the Toyota. We nodded at each other as we crouched low with our rifles extended as we moved toward the house.

The storm was providing us cover, but it was also making our approach to the old Victorian house difficult. The night that had descended was ebony black, and there wasn't any light from the house, and the farmyard light right next to the house was not lit. I was wondering if it was possible that the storm had knocked out the electricity. Or maybe the house was truly abandoned. The northern wind was battering us with almost knock out rain drops as they slammed into us. The hood of my rain slicker was still flapping so hard that it made it almost impossible to keep an eye on Nickey and the house at the same time. Our footing was suspect as the storm turned dirt into muck. I now had committed us to this assault, but I was starting to question my judgment. This entire trip to Lane County, Kansas may have been a terrible idea. If Nickey should get killed, well, I didn't even want to think about that. With the sideways rain, wind, no lights, and no moon, it was challenging to see the old Victorian house as we approached. When the lightning would flash, it would light up the entire sky, and we could see the house clearly then, but just for a few ticks of time. Shadows created by the blinding flashes of lightning were an unnerving sight. The shadows of each fence post, tree, abandoned farm equipment, and blade of tall grass created a haunting image as they danced and swayed in the gusting wind. The storm had made the surrounding landscape a surreal and eerie atmosphere like visions of one's nightmares.

Halfway in between the road and the house and at the tail end of a flash of lightning, I saw something. What? Had I just seen an orange and red momentary light from an upstairs window? I crouched low into the knee-high wet grass. The light had lasted just for a split-second, almost like a muzzle flash from a rifle. I had not heard a rifle report, but the thunder rolls were so loud it would have been impossible to hear them anyway. Were the lightning flashes and the ever-pirouetting shadows playing tricks on my mind? Looking eastward toward Nickey's position, I waited for another flash of lightning to see if she had also stopped her approach. As if on cue, the lightning produced a flickering strobe light effect. Nickey was not there! She was gone!

CHAPTER 35

Oh Shit! Nickey was no longer where she should be. Was I wrong? My heart raced as I waited for the next lightning bolt to light up the sky so I could once again check on her position. The storm provided the lighting; she was no longer there. Moving stealthily, but rapidly, I worked my way eastward through the knee-high wet grass to Nickey's last known position.

Anticipation and fear were making it difficult to move with caution, but I did so. It would help neither Nickey nor me if I got shot right now. Within a few minutes, I recollected I was where or close to where my wife should be. Slinging my rifle onto my back, I used both hands to part the wet and swaying grass to see if she had fallen. The rain, mud, wind, darkness, thick prairie grass, and the fact that Nickey was so small in stature would make it difficult to find the exact spot if she had. A bolt of lightning flashed and flickered for several seconds, and then I spotted her. I almost cried out in anguish. Nickey was down and not moving.
I fell to my knees next to her, and Nickey's eyes were shut. Placing my index and middle fingers on one side of Nickey's neck, just under her jaw, where her neck and jaw met, I felt no pulse. Or was there? My fingers were wet and muddy. Jamming them under my rain slicker, I wiped my fingers off on my shirt, clearing the mud and rain. I checked her pulse again. Closing my eyes and concentrating, I felt it! Tears welled in my eyes. She was alive!

WHEN THE SONG VANISHES

Nickey's eyes fluttered, and then they sprang open. Her face showed a grimace of pain as she said, "Shit! Someone shot me!"

The orange and red light I had seen in the window had been the muzzle flash of a rifle. Someone in the house had shot my wife. Bending closer to Nickey so she could see my face more clearly, "Where are you shot? How bad is it?"

Nickey was having difficulty breathing, and her voice wavered as she tried to speak, "Not sure. In my chest, I think. It hurts like hell!"

My eyes turned from her face, and I tried to see where she may have been shot. The darkness, swaying grass, and the dancing shadows made it difficult as I scanned her chest with just my eyes first, and then I ran my right hand over her chest. I felt it first before seeing it. They had shot her center of her chest, just in between her breasts. Panicked, I unzipped her vest and the high-caliber bullet had penetrated her ballistic vest. There was blood under the vest staining Nickey's shirt. As I opened her shirt, the bullet fell out. The bullet had penetrated, but just barely. Gingerly I buttoned up her blouse and zipped up the ballistic vest.

Fortunately, the Grand County ballistic vest had slowed it down enough that it had only nicked the skin. Unfortunately, the punch of being shot had taken her in the upper part of her ribcage that covered the heart. There was no doubt in my mind she had at least broken ribs. At worse, the broken ribs had nicked her heart or punctured a lung. Either way, Nickey needed to be looked at by someone who knew more about doctoring than I did.

I moved my head so I could look Nickey in the eyes. I said, "The ballistic vest slowed it down, so the bullet just nicked your skin. The reason you are having trouble breathing is no doubt at least broken ribs. You are out of this fight for now. It is for me to finish."

As a fresh round of lightning lit up the sky, Nickey said, "Bullshit!" As she tried to sit up, she grimaced again, and I could see her eyes go blank for a second as she almost passed out. Using my right hand behind my *Mi Vida's* back, I lay her back down into the mud. With my left hand, I took her Ruger Security-Six pistol from her holster and placed it in her hand. Looking Nickey in the eye, I then said, "You need to stay down until I come back for you. If anyone shows up, but me, you shoot them!"

Nickey nodded her head in pain and understanding, "Got it, Cowboy! Just so you know, when we get back to the motel - this is not a red-lace panty night."

Nickey, as always, faced with an extreme adversary, brought some light into the situation. Her comment made me laugh as I bent down and kissed my wife. Could this be our last kiss? I pushed that thought out of my mind.

With my rifle still slung on my back, I then grabbed Nickey's rifle, thinking I might need all the firepower I could muster. Whoever was in the house knew exactly where we were. Hoping not to get shot in the head, I slowly peeked over the swaying wet prairie grass toward the old Victorian house, gauging the distance. Maybe 50 yards? Half of a football field without covering fire.

Lightning flashed and a split-second later so did the orange muzzle flash of the rifle in the upstairs bedroom, and even in the thunder's roar, I could hear the bullet as it cut a scorching furrow into the right side of my cheek. Ducking and rolling to my right, I came back to my knees. Touching my new face wound, it was difficult with the pounding wetness of the rain and the darkness to know how badly I was bleeding. The wound felt deep. Whoever shot at me was a hell of a shot, for sure. Was it the radical Dan Minuex? All I truly knew was, another one half of an inch, I would have been a dead man.

I took a deep breath and took a few seconds to gather my thoughts and resolve. I realized that no matter what happens next. I was committed to this assault. There would be no retreat. In any retreat to carry Nickey out of here, I would have to stand to do so. Standing up was not an option currently. It would give the marksman in the old house a chance to finish us both off. Checking both rifles, I made sure that neither of the barrels had accidentally been packed with mud during my tuck-and-roll. My pistol was still in the holster, and my Kabar fighting knife was still sheathed. Still heavily armed, I formulated a plan in my mind. Maybe I could create my own cover fire? If the shooter had not moved from his high vantage point, I knew his location. Had he moved? If he had, my plan would only get me killed. Waiting until after the last flash of lightning to return to the black sky again, I peeked over the swaying knee-high grass. There was only one window on the second floor facing me. The shooter's advantage was tied to that one and only window. I was confident he was still there.

Dropping my head out of sight once again, I remembered my grandfather's words from the dream, *"Heed my words Dane, the one that got away is not done with you or the ones you love."* This ordeal needed to end tonight!

I crawled eastward through the wet grass and the mud. Even though soaked all the way through my clothing to my skin, I did not feel the chill of the rain. The adrenaline rush was keeping me alert and warm. My heart was pounding, but I felt in control. I felt I had gone roughly ten yards, and the mud was weighing me down. I had gone far enough.

Each rifle had a twenty-round magazine, a total of forty rounds to provide my cover fire as I moved toward the house. I had to get inside that house. Take the battle to close quarters. Once inside, if I made it that far, I knew it would be a crapshoot if I lived or died. It would be slow going tramping through the wet grass and mud for another forty yards; footing would be treacherous. Taking a deep breath, I cleared my mind of everything except for what was to become. Setting the hatred of Dan Minuex aside, I concentrated on all that surrounded me and focused my mind, bringing my Ute

Indian warrior heritage forward, drawing forth that killer instinct that lived deep within me.

After another deep breath, I quickly stood and fired all in one motion. The round from my M-14 carbine took out the pane of glass just above where the shooter was. "Yes, asshole, I can shoot too!"

Moving as fast as I could, firing every third or fourth step, I tried to zig and zag on my approach. The rain, mud, lightning flashes, and the tall grass were taking the zag out of my zig and was slowing me down. At this pace, I would be out of ammo in my rifles before I got to the house. Screw it! I just bee-lined it toward the front door, firing as I went. The shooter was keeping his head down as there was no return fire. Thirty-five yards…and then thirty yards…I was finding my stride. When I was about halfway to the house, my rifle failed to fire. Out of ammo, I tossed it aside and in almost the same motion swung the second rifle off my back and kept firing toward the upstairs window. Now twenty yards…and then ten yards. I ran out of ammo in the second rifle just as I had reached the front door. Tossing the M-14 aside, I drew my revolver in a practice maneuver, and with a full head of steam, I lowered my right shoulder and rammed the front door. Shit! The door didn't budge as I slammed into it.

Using my shoulder as a battering ram was the ultimate failure. I had bounced off and sprawled onto the front porch, and my Ruger pistol went spinning off the porch and out of sight. Trying not to pass out from the blow from the door, I tried to pull my Kabar fighting knife. My now broken right arm barely moved and was sprawled useless to my side. From the pain now radiating from not only my arm, but also my shoulder and collarbone, it would seem that my collarbone had also snapped. It would appear the door had kicked my ass. Just as I realized how bad the situation was, it got worse as the front door swung open, and Dan Minuex, the man responsible for the deaths of Laney, Rod, Isabella, and the others, stood there looking at me. Minuex slowly raised his 45 caliber Colt automatic pistol and took aim at my head. Knowing that death was just a hair trigger pull away, my only regret was that I had failed

WHEN THE SONG VANISHES

Nickey. I wished now I had never let her come with me. Minuex, without a smile and with no hurry in his voice, said, "Lee, I admit you and your wife have sand. You never gave up, and you kept after me. By coming here to Lane County, all you did was make it easier for me to get my revenge for my brother being killed."

The shot rang out, and it sounded deafening even with the thunder now in the distance. Then another round…and then another…until she had emptied her pistol. Minuex dropped his pistol and fell to his knees, looking beyond me. With the final realization of who had shot him, his expression went from confusion to understanding as he dropped face first on to the porch at my feet. There was no twitch, no movement at all. Dan Minuex was dead.

Rolling sluggishly onto my left shoulder, I looked behind me just as another round of lightning lit up the sky. Nickey Lynn Lee stood there looking like she was half drowned, hair wet, muddy, and tired, holding her now empty pistol. As she tried to holster her weapon, she fumbled and dropped it in the mud. She looked at it lying there and then looked at me and rolled her eyes as if saying to herself, "Screw it." Leaving the pistol in the mud, Nickey moved slowly toward the front porch. She was struggling to breathe from the broken ribs as she struggled to walk up the three steps of the porch. Trying to kneel, *Mi Vida* collapsed on me, bringing a grimace of pain to both of our faces. She brought her face within inches of mine, and we searched each other's eyes as she said, "Cowboy, trying to bust open the door like that was gallant, brave, and heroic, but incredibly stupid!"

Just before our lips touched, I said, "No, shit, Sherlock!"

CHAPTER 36

On the night that Nickey killed Dan Minuex, even though both of us had been severely injured, we somehow made it back to our Toyota Land Cruiser and drove back to Dighton. We presented ourselves to the authorities of the Lane County Sheriff's department. Our story to the local authorities included that they could find one of the FBI's number one fugitives dead at the house in Pendennis. After they had seen the extent of our injuries, the sheriff's department had us transported to the nearest trauma center, which was an hour away in Garden City, Kansas. Once at the hospital, Nickey and I were promptly handcuffed to our hospital beds until the sheriff could investigate our story.

My collarbone was reset, but my arm required surgery and the insertion of some screws to hold the bones in place so it could begin to heal and make me whole again. I was still handcuffed to the bed when the nurses wheeled me into the operating room. Although seriously injured with three broken ribs after being shot, Nickey did not require surgery, just some painkillers to ease the throb of her injuries.
The next several days after the fatal confrontation with Dan Minuex were a whirlwind of activity as the Lane County Sheriff's Department was contemplating if they should charge Nickey and me with a misdemeanor of trespassing or to press murder charges

against the both of us in the death of Dan Minuex. It was not until the national media and FBI Special Agent Ken Ekross showed up at the hospital that all that talk of charging Nickey and me with any crime was formally dismissed, and the handcuffs came off.

The family of Dan Minuex lay him to rest next to his brother Mitch and other members of the Insurgence in the Dighton Cemetery east of town in a quiet family only service. The media kept a respectable distance as the family exited the funeral without speaking with any of them.

The following week was total chaos for Nickey and me as the media hounded us to do interviews in the death's wake of the final Insurgence member Dan Minuex. Once the doctors said Nickey and I could be released, Special Agent Ekross snuck us out in the middle of the night past the sleeping reporters in the hospital's lobby and took us back to Dighton to retrieve our Toyota Land Cruiser for our trip back home to Grand County.

After returning home to Granby and Grand County, for the following two weeks, Nickey and I were recovering from our injuries at home. Worried and loving family and friends came to visit. Sheriff Tom Walker came to visit several times. In the beginning, Tom was not happy with either of us for going on a manhunt out of Grand County's jurisdiction. Nickey and I finally relented and gave one interview to John Lindsey of Channel 7 News, which was aired on a Friday night across the United States during prime time. The media talking heads said that Nickey and I were heroes of the highest order. With the Grand County Sheriff's department being portrayed in a positive light, Sheriff Walker softened his stance. It was tough for Tom to be upset with us, and his attitude toward Nickey and me returned to normal.

Nickey's injuries healed faster than mine, and she could return to full duty two weeks to the day after Minuex had shot her, and she had shot him. It would not be until another three weeks before I got a work release for desk duty only.

My first day back to work, Nickey had to drive since my right arm was still in a cast. I was feeling good about being home and going back to the job that I loved. *Mi Vida* looked beautiful this morning as the rising sun shone on her face as she drove. Her smile was radiant. There was not a cloud in the sky, and the air was clean and crisp with a slight chill to it. It was a good day to be in Grand County, the Rocky Mountains, and with the woman whom I loved. It felt like a John Denver song. Reaching into the glove compartment, I found the cassette tape I was looking for and plugged in John Denver's collection of songs from his album, "Back Home Again." One of my favorites started to play and Nickey and I sang along to the ballad named "Sweet Surrender."

I don't know where I'm going,
I'm not sure where I've been.
There's a spirit that guides me, a light that shines for me,
My life is worth the living, I don't need to see the end.

When we got to the office and got out of the Grand County Sheriff's Blazer, Nickey fast scooted by me and hustled to the front door. She quickly opened the door for me. With a dramatic wave of her hand as if she was ushering me in, she said, "I know this door sticks some and thought it was best to get it open for you so that you don't have another 'incident' with a door that does not open easily."

Nickey's smile was as big as I have ever seen it as I walked through the door. Passing her, I said, "Hilarious, smartass."

There were the usual greetings and well wishes of all that were there, welcoming me back to work. It felt good to be back in the sheriff's department among my co-workers, but a little sad remembering those that who lost their lives. Walking past the empty desks of those who had died, I felt a small sense of relief knowing that Minuex had paid for what he and the others had done.

WHEN THE SONG VANISHES

Less than a minute had passed since sitting down at my desk when the phone rang. Time to get to work. Clearing my thoughts of the well wishes, I answered it on the second ring. "This is Undersheriff Dane Lee. How can I assist you today?"

There was static on the line as if they made the call from a great distance. It was several seconds before the voice on the other end hissed, *"Dane Lee?"*

The call was confusing with the crackle and pop of static. Concentrating, I could not decipher if the poor connection caused the "hiss" or not. Answering the question, I said, "Yes, this is Dane Lee."

Finally, the static cleared. Then the unnerving voice of a dead man spoke, *"Soon Dane, I am coming for you and her, and the baby!"* The static had cleared, but the "hiss" in the voice remained. A chill shivered up and down my spine as the voice on the other end of the line hissed as if in an echo chamber. It was a voice I had not heard in over a year.

The line went dead as the person on the other end hung up. Nickey, who had been sitting at her desk, looked at me and her eyes showed concern when she asked, "What? You look like you just saw a ghost!"

I ran the words through my mind trying to comprehend what they meant or even if I had heard them at all. *"Soon Dane, I am coming for you and her, and the baby!"*

Slowly I laid the phone down onto its cradle, and I looked at Nickey. "I didn't see a ghost, I just heard one!"

Nickey's face now showed confusion on top of her concern as she stood and crossed the room and lay her hand gently on my shoulder. "Are you okay? What do you mean you just heard a ghost?"

Looking my wife straight in the eye and in an unsure voice, "That phone call; it sounded just like Samael Amos!"

Nickey, without thinking, slowly reached up and touched the scar on her face that Samael Amos had inflicted on her and said in confusion, "What? How can that be? Amos is dead! Bones scattered to the winds!"

Throughout my life, I had been fearless in all that I did. The phone call had rattled me; it had put a scare into me. Scared not for myself, but for my wife and the... wait? His words *"Soon Dane, I am coming for you and her, and the baby!"* echoed in my mind again. The malevolent voice had said... baby!

Nickey, still looking deep into my soul, asked, "What did he say?"

Without hesitation and just above a whisper, I answered, "Amos said, *'Soon Dane, I am coming for you and her, and the baby!'"*

Nickey stumbled and almost fell as she sat down hard in the wooden chair next to my desk. Her eyes swelled with tears as she spoke, "How did he know? No one knows!"

Now it was my turn to be confused. "How did he know what?" Nickey's face now showed fear as she told me, "I was going to tell you tonight after dinner! Dane, I am pregnant!"

Kurt James

WHEN THE SONG VANISHES

An original song written
By
Kurt James

Long Days, Lonely Nights

Can't count the miles
Or the months of emptiness
Shed a million tears
I recall the sound of your voice
When you told me goodbye
I said darlin', you're makin' a big mistake
As you walked out the door
Falling apart
Is what I do best
Counting the miles
Of all the emptiness
Millions of tears
That I have shed
With the voices of memories
Singing in my head

Falling apart is what I do best
Counting the scars of all my broken mess
The pain and the doubt and the loneliness
Falling apart is what I do best

Darling
It's a mistake
Walking out the door
Please don't take
Our love
And shake it
To the core
It will be the long days
And the lonely nights

And it will be us
No more
Please don't take our love
Walking out the door

Falling apart is what I do best
Counting the scars of all my broken mess
The pain and the doubt and the loneliness
Falling apart is what I do best

Matt Lee – Mountain Man

Dane Lee's grandfather Matt Lee was first introduced in the Kurt James western adventure Rocky Mountain Ghost. Here is a sampling from Chapter 5 of that book which is available on Amazon.

Rocky Mountain Ghost
By
Kurt James

It almost felt good to talk about it after all these years. Clearing my throat, I began again, "That morning that Tom Driscoll had faded into the wilderness, the five of us began to talk at length and with more seriousness about going to find the La Caverna Del Oro. It was an adventure for the young and as it turned out for the not so very bright.

That morning during breakfast we all began to recall the clues that Driscoll had laid out in his tale about the location of the cave of gold. We knew it was roughly 150 miles west of us in the Spanish Peaks region and supposedly on the newly named Marble Mountain. After making a pact, the five of us decided to give it one summer to look for the lost cave and to see if the legend was true. After deciding that was what we were going to do, we wasted no time in informing our employers William Bent and Ceran St. Vrain we would be leaving. And with a halfhearted laugh, we told them we would be back for trapping season penniless and broke looking for work. They assured us we would be welcomed back with open arms.

Being used to having to pack our mounts in a hurry, we were able to head west and into the unknown about midday. We were jovial and in high spirits. It was good to be on such an adventure with those that could easily be your brothers.

All I recall about the trip to Marble Mountain was that it went well and after about eight days or so we found ourselves camping at the base of Marble Mountain. The country and the lay of the land were new to us, but it was still the Rocky Mountains and all five of us lived and breathed the Rockies.

From our vantage point as we rode from the east, we could tell that the top of Marble Mountain was well above where the trees never grew anymore. Possibly 3,000 feet or more above timberline. According to the tale, as it was told by old man Driscoll, the cave of gold was located just above timberline and on the southwest side of the face of the mountain. With no other clue to go by and all of us knowing this was probably a folly and a one in a million chance, we were nonetheless game and ready for the adventure. We headed to the southwest side of Marble Mountain.

KURT JAMES

It was on the third or fourth day of exploring the southwest side that I started to see the crows. Never more than one at a time and I was never sure if it was the same crow or not, but it or they seemed to be watching us. I brought it up to the others at supper and they laughed at me and kidded me for being scared of my own shadow. Of course, I laughed it off also with my friends, but when Sam began to play his harmonica that evening, I could not shake the feeling that we were being watched from close and afar. I had difficulty sleeping that night because the sounds of the woods and timber were different, I could not put my finger on it, but the sounds of the wilderness had changed. I kept my new Hawkins rifle close and the powder under the buffalo robe I used for sleeping to keep it dry. My gut instinct was telling me something was off kilter in the woods that surrounded us.

The next morning after some dried venison jerky for breakfast, we set out again to explore and Mike Sands saw it first and yelled for all of us to come running. What he discovered was an ancient fortress at the mouth of a small cave. And I mean ancient like 300 years before ancient. The walls of the fort were constructed of rock and timbers, and rifle pits had been constructed for its defense, which led all five of us to suspect that Driscoll's story of the Spanish legend and the three monks was in fact a true telling of an antique but not forgotten story.

Dan Buxman found an old, tarnished brass Spanish helmet and breastplate and handed the breast plate to me with a huge grin. I could not help but notice it had a hole in it roughly where the heart of the person that had been wearing it would have been.
Since the ancient fort we found was just below timberline and according to the tale told by the old man Driscoll, the La Caverna Del Oro was above timberline, we set out to explore above the old fort. Once again, a crow or "the" crow landed in an evergreen directly in front of me and watched me as I rode by him. Now looking back after all these years, I now know it was a warning and I did not have the wherewithal to understand it then. With an odd feeling of dread, I continued on and upwards with my friends.

WHEN THE SONG VANISHES

Within a couple of hours, Jay Edwards had found the entrance to a much larger cave. As we all bunched up to check out the cave, we were excited and more than positive it was La Caverna Del Oro - the Spanish lost cave of gold. There was a faded but apparent red Maltese cross marking the entrance to the cave. We were all dumbfounded, knowing there was a small chance of ever finding the cave, but here we were, and destiny had led us straight to it. We were obviously jovial, laughing, and punching each other in the arms about our find, but since it was well past midday and we were all hungry, we decided to make camp at the entrance and fry up some venison steaks and beans from our supplies. The others spoke of what they would do with our newly found riches even though we actually had not found any gold yet. I was quiet and reserved with the feeling of dread overpowering me. I kept my eyes on the tree lines surrounding our camp. We had tied our horses and pack horses to a picket line in between two trees and I kept an eye on them also.

After a filling supper of venison steak, Sam Walters broke out his harmonica and started to play a merry tune. I tried to join in the festivities of the moment, but I failed as I remembered something the old man Tom Driscoll had said and that we all had seemed to forget. Others believe that the Indians now protect the mountain and the demon cave after being directed by their "Great Spirit" to stop anyone from ever stepping foot in the cave again.
Remembering this part of the tale, I felt that overwhelming sense of foreboding again and decided to bring it up to the others as soon as Sam's merry rendition on his harmonica was over.
It turned out sooner than ole' Sam and the rest of us ever imagined as an arrow pierced his throat dead center of his arms as they were raised holding and playing his harmonica. The remaining four of us were slow in moving as we were all in some sort of shock momentarily as we watched Sam gurgle on his own blood and paw at the killing arrow in his throat.

The next to go down was Dan Buxman as more Indians than I could count stormed our small encampment; Dan took a lance through the back that pierced him through and through.
Maybe because I had been on edge already because my gut instinct had told me things were off kilter, I had my Hawkins rifle loaded and primed, and I shot and killed the Indian that had killed poor Dan.

Out of the corner of my eye, I saw Jay Edwards taken off his feet as two of the wild Injuns tackled him; he really never had a chance as they went to work on him with their killing tomahawks.
Mike Sands and I were also attacked by numerous hostiles, and we were giving them all they wanted with our tomahawks and skinning knives. In the initial onslaught, I had cut and cleaved two, and Mike had taken down three as we fought for our lives in front of the La Caverna Del Oro.

We had a few moments to catch our breaths and after the first rush of hostiles, we looked at each other knowing this was our day to die, and we nodded at each other as only friends can do in the face of certain death. Death awaited us and as true warriors, we knew that we were not going to make it easy for those that wanted us dead. Taking my weapons and swinging my arms back and forth in front of me to limber up, I was ready and even willing as the next wave of hostiles rushed in at us.

Covered in blood and not really knowing if it was ours or theirs and with our Hawkins now useless and forgotten in the battle, we fought like savages and madmen slashing and hammering with our skinning knives and tomahawks. I lost count of how many Indians we either killed or maimed in those moments of blood lust and at the height of the battle in front of the demon cave. All the while during the blood, killing, and slaughter, we were being pushed back closer and closer to the entrance to the cave.

I saw Mike go down to one knee as one of the hostiles was able to hit him at the top of his shoulder with a tomahawk. Seeing my friend and brother Mike still fighting from this now almost defenseless position, I fought and killed my way to his side and was able to grab him and lift him back to his feet. Out of the corner of my eye, I saw the darkness of the cave and I grabbed Mike and rushed headlong into the darkness and the entrance of the La Caverna Del Oro."

KURT JAMES

Kurt James was born and raised in the foothills of the Colorado Rocky Mountains. Kurt's family roots were from western Kansas and having lived in South Dakota for 20 years, Kurt naturally had become an old western and nature enthusiast. Over the years Kurt has become one of Colorado's prominent nature photographers through his brand name of Midnight Wind Photography. The Denver Post, PM Magazine, and 9NEWS in Denver, Colorado featured his poetry. Kurt is also a feature writer for HubPages and Creative Exiles with the article's focused on Colorado history, ghost towns, outlaws, and poetry. Inspired at a young age by writers such as Jack London, Louis L'Amour, and Max Brand have formed Kurt's natural ability as a storyteller. Kurt has published 16 books all based in and around the Colorado Rocky Mountains. Using the Midnight Wind Publishing brand, Kurt James novels, short stories, reference books, and poetry, are available in print or download on Amazon, Barnes and Noble, Goodreads, and other fine bookstores. And a few shady bookstores as well. Kurt has 3 books that he is currently writing. The 8th book in his Rocky Mountain Series - Raphael Eye for an Eye. His third ghost town reference book, Kansas Ghost Towns, Hauntings, Treasure Tales, and Other BS. And a western/horror novel - Devil's Tower Spirit of Chiha Tanka. Kurt is a proud member of Western Writers of America.